Gillyflower

Gillyflower

A NOVEL

Diane Wald

SHE WRITES PRESS

Published April 2019
Printed in the United States of America
Print ISBN: 978-1-63152-517-9
E-ISBN: 978-1-63152-518-6
Library of Congress Control Number: 2018956295

For information, address:
She Writes Press
1563 Solano Ave #546
Berkeley, CA 94707

Interior design by Tabitha Lahr

She Writes Press is a division of SparkPoint Studio, LLC.

In memory of
James Twyford Mehorter

"Dreams and anguish bring us together."

—Eugène Ionesco

1. Nora

The pain is essentially gone, but the mystery remains. I went through all the proper stages of grief—denial, anger, bargaining, depression, and acceptance—sometimes one by one, sometimes simultaneously, but I never did get past the wonder of it. A death would have been easier to endure. For my situation—ours—there exists no comforting ritual, no consolation from relatives or friends, no body of literature that could interpret or advise. The one person with whom I might have shared my loss was the one person whom I could never contact—oh, he was alive, and reachable had I attempted to reach him, but that was unthinkable. Somewhere in the world he was struggling just as I was, in his own (and, I was quite sure, better) way. I have wonderful memories, it's true; I will always have them. But try as I might to focus on their sweetness, any sweetness always seems to lie, tantalizingly, at center-bottom of a clear, but immeasurably deep, pool of bewilderment.

Let me set things in time: It was 1984. I'd read in the paper that Hugh had been presented with a prestigious award for a new film. The article quoted his very amusing acceptance speech, but there was no photograph. The other papers did not carry one either; I know because I went out and bought them all. I'd considered whether or not to even see the film, knowing I suppose all the time that I would go see it, sooner or later. I knew, too, what would happen when I did: how my heart would thunder against my ribs, drowning out the soundtrack; how my eyes would throb, exhausted from their effort to absorb his every move; and how my mind would thrill to judge and catalogue each shot, not in order to criticize his performance but in an effort to determine: Was he well? Would he live forever? It was not enough to understand that his work would outlast us all; I had to be sure of his continued, actual presence in the world.

All of this is not to say that my life was a ruin, that my every energy was directed toward nourishing the memory of Hugh in my arms, or even that I was—or ever had been—truly "in love" with him in the usual sense. I was what is known as happily married; I had a decent job, good friends, and in recent years my drawings had sold nicely, earning me a small but satisfying reputation. It is not to say either that I did not almost constantly, under the surface of my conscious life, continue to mull over the things that had happened, or that I did not think of him every day. It might have been better to forget, but I was unwilling.

Since I knew I would never find an explanation for what had happened to Hugh and me, the question itself was what I held to, and I tried to make it part of me, to "pray without ceasing," as mystics do, until my very breath was the question, an involuntary impulse I could rely upon to sustain my need. The only thing I was sure of: Hugh was not a dream. He had been one once, but could never be again. Keeping that in mind, I believed I was luckier than most.

I guess I knew something would happen when I wrote that letter, although of course I told myself nothing ever would. Before I wrote it, I had that feeling you get when the inevitable is dropping down around you, and it's not the fact that you can't stop it that bothers you, it's that you feel you ought to want to stop it but you wouldn't if you could.

The idea for the letter hit me while I was driving home from New York. The day before I'd seen Hugh in a Broadway play, and I was still trying to recover from what had happened in that theater. My elation, my feeling of having been truly graced by guardian angels, was marred only by an absurd and gnawing sense of shame regarding my role in the incident. Not that I was sorry for what I'd done.

I should explain a few things. Hugh Sheenan is an actor, a movie star. An Irishman, raised in Canada, who'd made his home in England for many years. Even his Irishness appealed to me: my mother's maiden name is Feeney. I'd had a crush on him as far back as I could remember, a mighty crush considering I was never the crush type and he was never all that popular, except for one or two brilliant but not overwhelmingly well-reviewed films. He was what people call an actor's actor, but in spite of his astonishing good looks (especially, some say, when he was young, though I am not among them), I think he was rather a hard man for most fans to love. Very tall, spare, dark of hair and eye, heroic, witty, with a reputation for drink and wildness, Hugh nevertheless remained somewhat aloof from his audiences and somewhat untouchable by the press. He allowed them to observe him, and to say what they would, but he never, shall we say, invited them home to tea. One got the impression that he could happily go on practicing his profession on some luminous star in the heady altitudes of art, looking on both adulation and adverse criticism as necessary, but satellite, planets. His intensity caught at my heart—his intensity and his eyes.

Experienced, baroque, heavy-lidded, ever so slightly angry, his eyes radiated a passion and power that made me weak and grateful even when I was watching one of his lesser films. His eyes are black—truly black, not dark brown. The color is clear, with a glint of blue at times, but elusive and often shocking. For years I'd had pictures of Hugh Sheenan on my bulletin board and had always gone out of my way to see his movies and to read things about him, even in the shoddier magazines. However ridiculous the story, just reading his name gave me pleasure. Never did I think I'd get to see him in person; as far as I knew, he rarely left his home in London to come to the States. When he did come he was making movies, and what chance would I ever have to catch him at that? I can't say it really mattered: he fell into the category of an "if-you-ever-met-him-he-could-never-measure-up" celebrity, well outside the realm of everyday life.

Then one day my younger sister, Fran, came to visit from New York (Fran and my mother both lived there, in the house we'd all shared before my father died). We were in my study and she looked at the tacked-up photo of Hugh over my desk and said, "That's a great photograph. Have you read the reviews of his new play? They're really good."

It took a minute to sink in; I couldn't believe what I was hearing. "What play?" I asked.

I must have looked funny because Fran laughed and said, "My God, don't tell me you didn't know Hugh Sheenan is making a month-long appearance on Broadway in *The Lion's Share*? It just opened."

I tortured her for details, of which she had few. Then I called my mother and begged her to get tickets, telling her I'd drive down from Boston any weekend that month, or if weekends were sold out, any time at all—somehow I'd get the time off from work. Mom said she'd like to go herself and promised to call me back the next day.

That night I dreamed of Hugh, but it was a puzzling dream. The scene was lifted from one of his recent films (rather a flop, though rather endearing). He appeared to be meditating up on the roof of a church. There was something wonderful in that simple moonlit set: Hugh, sprawled on a pitched shingle roof in a loose white shirt, leaning back on his elbow with a wistful, mysterious look on his face and his fabulous eyes shining with something that can only be described, oxymoronically, as happy grief. I was standing on the lawn below, looking up at him, and at first, he had no idea anyone was there. He continued to muse and I continued to stare, and then finally the power of the stare made him look down. Our eyes caught, hard; the impact stunned me. I woke up. My first thought was to wonder if my mother had had any luck.

I went to work but by ten o'clock I was going crazy, so I called her. Not only had she obtained matinee tickets for the Sunday most convenient for me, but she had gotten first-row seats. They were hideously expensive, but I didn't care. I called my husband at his office to see if he wanted to go, but he said he couldn't leave town that weekend and to offer his ticket to my sister. (Rick knew I was nuts about Hugh; he called me "Miss Number-One Fan.")

When there were still three weeks before the play, I began a countdown, getting more excited by the hour. Though grateful for my mother's help with the tickets, and grateful to my sister for setting off the whole chain of action, in a way I wished I were going alone. My mother's oldest (and most annoying) friend, Belinda, was coming too; she and my mother liked to go out together, since both of their husbands had died.

As the time drew near, I entered a very fanciful state. I bought a weird and lovely yellow silk dress to wear to the performance and planned my drive and weekend meticulously. I bought pale yellow stockings to match the dress and took really good care of myself those weeks, as if preparing for a wedding or some other life-altering occasion. I modeled the dress for Rick, who sweetly told me, "It makes you look like a flower."

When the day came to leave for New York, I was calm, I felt prepared. I drove to my mother's on the Saturday, and when I went to bed that night in my old room I dreamed the conclusion of the rooftop dream: it shook me to return to it. This time Hugh tumbled from his rooftop in slow motion, his body tumbling over and over and the white shirt loosening from his body like a great flying scarf. He landed near me, in the same leaning posture he'd been in on the roof, and was obviously unhurt. We looked into one another. People began to gather, acting as if they were going to take him away. "He's mine," I cried out. "He's mine." They fled, and we were alone. For what seemed like years, we stared into each other's eyes—it was like falling through the deepest sky, without a consciousness of any other state.

I woke feeling scared and delighted, my limbs returning to the waking world slowly, tingling with possibilities, as if they'd just been born.

2. Hugh

My birthday had again arrived (I was sure I'd had one just a few months before), and I was in a bad mood. The play was going well. I was able to see my four-year-old daughter, on loan from my ex-wife, as frequently as I liked, and she, lovely child, did not appear to hate me. Even the early-summer New York weather was not at all hideous, and I had to admit I'd probably be suffering more had I been in London. Yet suffer I did. I was aging like a cheap wine; I was a living cliché. That morning I looked in the bathroom mirror and said, "Sheenan, you are fifty-seven today and you look seventy. Your teeth are nearly the color of sand; your gums have receded another foot at least. The lines on your forehead are as deep as fjords." I took a whack at my ridiculous black, brown, grey, and blond hair (having been dyed so many times, for so many roles, my hair could no longer decide what color to be) but could not whack it into order. I shaved with my trusty straightedge and took a chunk off one of my famous cheekbones. Bugger.The blood dripped into my mouth and I had to staunch it with paper toweling. Stepping into my shorts, I tore them. They were new. My favorite shirt had somehow become bloodied from the razor attack, so I put on a striped one that made me look like a sports referee of some sort, matched it poorly to an emerald green bow-tie, and hitched on some trousers. Noticed I'd lost more weight. Could find only one of my lucky blue gloves. Shouted for coffee.

"No coffee, darlin'." The shout was returned by my faithful pit-bull secretary, Leon. I was not allowed coffee. Not allowed spirits of any sort. Not allowed spicy or fatty foods or any kind of physical pleasure whatsoever, though I did manage to smoke my beloved Galoises whenever I could find a secret space in which to indulge. I think Leon was afraid to stop me, and Leon was not afraid of much. When he did carp about my smoking, I always quoted to him the words of the old music-hall song: "A little bit of what you fancy does you good." But, as I said, he did not offer much resistance to my habit; since my second wife had evaporated, I had chased after nary a woman, had not really even desired any, and possibly Leon felt a messy trail of tobacco grains preferable to a messier trail of females in my bed. As it was, I slept little.

Leon brought in my treacle and gruel—or whatever it was. Since they'd revamped my heart's valves and my entire circulatory network some years earlier, imposing the strictest and most diabolical dietary restrictions upon me, I'd simply eaten whatever Leon offered, growling and griping to make him feel needed, though in truth I cared very little anymore what I ate.

"Leon," I said that morning, "as you know, it is my birthday, and I'll thank you not to offer your condolences, congratulations, or advice. Hold all calls. I'll be going to the theater early, in the blue car."

Sensing my mood, Leon said only that he'd call for the car to come 'round in half an hour.

I liked the blue car, an older American thing belonging to a friend in the city who kindly offered me the use of it when I was in the States. It came with a driver who was, happily, a man of few words, and it permitted me more privacy than the limousine the theater provided. Not that I was all that famous anymore; indeed, by this point I think it was more my bizarre appearance that attracted attention than my once-well-known face. Once they'd noticed me, people would sometimes recognize me, but few of them bothered with me other than to comment to their friends on how poorly, or how old, or perhaps simply how odd I looked—if they could even remember my name, that is. I imagined that they stared at me in pity; I was rife with pity for myself. Tall as a giraffe, thin as a weed, I saw myself flapping through the city like a vision of death and doom and felt I must appear that way to others. So I habitually skulked to the theater in the blue car, shuffling in through a side door, and not shuffling out again until an hour after the show, when I would skedaddle to some boring restaurant (preapproved by Leon) or back to the hotel for an insipid meal in my room. I felt like nothing so much as an aging rock crab . . . "a pair of ragged claws/ Scuttling across the floors of silent seas." Eliot, you wry dog.

But the play, as I said, was going well. I was even enjoying it. My costar was a talented, daffy, and quirky-looking young man whose high spirits were often infectious, and the rest of the cast was likewise talented and benign. Truly I had my run of the place—they allowed me liberties with the script I wouldn't have allowed myself—but then it was my first Broadway appearance, and as a staple of the British stage and bona fide curiosity of a movie star, I was filling the house almost every performance.

Thinking back, I was a man in a trance. Had I been younger (pre-surgery younger) I would have taken to drink, but a drink here and there was all I could handle at that time, and even here and there was not that enjoyable. There remained a little post-surgical pain, which positioned itself for some perverse reason in the general vicinity of my gut and not my chest. I think a lifetime of heart-highs and heartaches had steeled the contents of my chest cavity to a certain level of activity. I relied on my past reputation, my impeccable brandy-swirling style, and a flamboyant pantomime with my cigarette holder to make me look a drunk, and was often rewarded for this successfully rendered minor role by a finger-shaking reference in the next day's gossip column: "Hugh Sheenan seen swaggering and staggering at Milty's. Didn't we hear the old dear daren't down a drop?" the writer would cunningly say, and, if I were lucky, there'd also be a smudged photo of me wiping my brow with my white silk scarf. Never taking the time to properly cleanse my ruined features after the play, I had ravaged quite a few scarves with makeup, much to poor Leon's dismay. He was a wonderful mother.

So after the performance on my birthday, which had occasioned a pleasing ovation and a rowdy singing of the happy-birthday song at play's end, I tootled away the requisite hour, then called for the blue car. I told Leon I wanted to go to Milty's, but he said, "The Tall Ship, Mr. Sheenan; I think tonight you should have white fish."

"'Mr. Sheenan,' is it, Leon? And what infringement of the rules have I unwittingly committed this evening?"

"None, Mr. Sheenan," said Leon with a sassy grin. "I just thought you would appreciate a little extra respect on your birthday."

I did laugh at that. I loved Leon. If he'd been a woman I would have married him years ago, and I often told him so. It made him grimace but I know it pleased him. Leon knew when I needed a giggle, he wiped up after me, he put up with almost anything, and probably he would have done even had he not been so handsomely paid. I'd met him during my disastrous season in the Royal Navy and had kept him by me ever since.

I told people Leon had rescued me from a dreadful death at sea, but the truth was that it was I who rescued him, during our brief foreign travels in the Queen's service, from the clutches of a beautiful and wicked girl who was simply not worthy of his virtues. In fact, I bought her off, at a dear price, and Leon never knew it, nor did he know that before he fell for her she'd fallen for me and that his purest of hillside flowers and I had spent three thoroughly drunken and dissipated days in a fleabag hotel. The woman had a truly beastly outlook on life, even for my taste in those days. When I flicked her off she went after Leon, which only shows what a dolt the girl was to begin with; any clear-sighted woman would have been able to perceive his worth over mine in the flash of an eye. I was not even famous then, so there was really no excuse for her at all.

At The Tall Ship I surprised my surprise party by going immediately to the gents and slipping out the back way to head for Milty's in the nearest cab. Once there I ordered whiskey and something with a heavy sauce over a pungent red meat and settled down for an indulgent hour before being discovered by Leon and the loyal leftovers from the small party; they had followed my trail to Milty's in order to force me to enjoy the celebration of my imminent demise. I did indeed feel that my demise was more imminent than usual that night because, no doubt owing to my imprudent choice of entree, my stomach was having a rather raucous party of its own. My skinflint heart would simply not allow itself to pump forth the wherewithal for any extra digestive energy, birthday or no.

Leon took me home after testing my damp and trembling brow with his cool, steady hand, dosed me with the most potent of his English-born remedies, and put me to bed in flannels. He had a little leather case of medications that he had cajoled my London medics into entrusting to him (they didn't want to risk giving over my care to colonials) and the longest list of instructions for their administration I had ever seen. At times I almost delighted in feeling ill, such were dear Leon's histrionics.

Whatever he gave me that night certainly did the trick. Not only did the pain in my stomach immediately cease, but I lost all feeling below the waist in a matter of minutes. I was lightheaded and feeling most lovely, and my last conscious thought before falling headfirst into a deep, salty tide pool of sleep was that death might be beautiful if one could die simultaneously with achieving one single instant of perfect, unbidden harmony with another soul. Even in my doped-up state, I remember thinking that that was a very peculiar goal, not to mention its being rather an awkward one to realize.

And, as the old song goes, that night I dreamed the strangest dream. I was on the set of a film I had recently made in California, doing a scene in which I was positioned on the roof of a small frame church, musing under the moon. In the film, that's all there is to it, but in the dream I dreamed that night I fell off the roof, slowly, tumbling over and over in the air and feeling my shirt loosen and flap and rewrap itself around me, a miniature shroud. (Even as the dream progressed, my conscious mind wondered about the shirt: was this a dream prescient of my death?) I landed, finally, unhurt upon the grass, and looked up into the eyes of a young woman I did not know. I looked at her for a long, long time, and thereby came to know her. She was not beautiful but she had hypnotized me, and when I woke up I felt extremely lonely.

3. Nora

Belinda drove us all into the city early that afternoon, and after diddling about looking for a perfect place to park her beloved Saab, we found we had over an hour to kill before the theater would open. (This was, of course, my fault, for in my panic lest we be late I had shepherded everyone out the door when they were barely dressed.) It was a nice afternoon, not too hot, not too crowded, and we strolled about for a while, just four women on the town, taking the necessary photographs of each other and voraciously window shopping.

At last we could stroll no more, and we found ourselves in an expensive theater-district deli, complete with theatrically made-up fifty-year-old waitress, ten-dollar-per-person minimum, and out-of-order restrooms. The management had, however, considerately arranged for its customers to avail themselves of the restrooms in a bar across the alley, and there I proceeded, needing a moment alone before the big event and suffering somewhat from caffeine nerves and a grossly rich carrot cake, prescribed by my sister for what she called my "galloping fan syndrome." I guess she thought having a lump in my stomach would calm me down, but the sugar made my head spin.

I took as long as I decently could in the stall, and as I washed and looked in the mirror, I looked into the face of a stranger. The new silk dress was fine, my hair was okay, there were no runs in my stockings, and the effect created by my long seashell earrings was, I thought, very nice indeed. But the face, the face was wrong—it seemed not to be mine at all. The eyes were strangely shining, slightly sunken; the mouth was a little drawn and very pale; and, oddest of all, the face looked ageless—not youthful in an attractive way, or mature in a meaningful way, but flat and funny, like a face in a second-rate pastel portrait done on a boardwalk. I tried to fix it up a little with lipstick and blush, but I couldn't effect much change.

So at last we sat in our front-row seats: my mother on the aisle, then me, Belinda, and Fran. The edge of the stage was less than six feet away, on a plane just above my shoulders. The curtains rose and I fell headlong into the play—a familiar one I'd read before. Nearly ten minutes elapsed before Hugh made his first appearance, and when the audience applauded his entrance I was shocked, having forgotten altogether where I was.

But there *he* was. It was like seeing an old, dear friend. He did not look well, but he looked commanding; he was phenomenally thin and terribly tall. His hair was very short and, oddly, multicolored. He was wearing a dark coat and leaning back on his heels and rocking back and forth with the rhythm of his lines. As he walked toward the front of the stage his onyx eyes beamed out over the auditorium, stilling everyone, and when he smiled they lit up like rockets. His smile would have melted the Ice Queen herself, and I was touched to see that, up close, his teeth were less than perfect. I settled into my seat in bliss, thanking the playwright silently for having written long speeches for Hugh's character in almost every scene. I reveled in his voice, in the soothing theatrical cadences, in every nuance of his performance, trying desperately to chisel each moment into my mind to remember from that day on.

At intermission, Belinda couldn't shut up. She was all a-dither, flapping about in her seat like a sparrow in a dust bath. "God, he's so marvelous," she gushed. "But doesn't he look older than you thought he would?"

"He's fifty-six or -seven," I said.

My mother looked at me. "How do you know that?"

"I read it somewhere," I said.

Fran looked over at me and winked. What was she winking for? I wondered, resenting her conspiratorial air at the same time I welcomed her congenial intention. Hugh was my private business.

"Well, he's fabulous, fabulous, blah, blah, blah," everyone babbled on, and I tuned them out and left them to discuss things. My sister went out for a cigarette, but though I needed one desperately myself, I found I couldn't join her; all I wanted was for the play to begin again, though I knew that would only rush its inevitable ending. I'd probably never have the opportunity to see Hugh Sheenan again, and even if by some miracle I did see him in another play, or even catch a glimpse of him on the street in the city, it would never feel like today.I was so very happy.

It was near the end of the final act when it happened. Having read the play before, I knew the last scene was coming up quickly, and while I had barely taken my eyes from Hugh the whole play through, for the past ten minutes or so I had been concentrating on his every facial gesture, fairly memorizing his face, so eager was I to give my inebriated brain every possible chance to keep that face alive forever.

Our seats were nearest the left of the set, and there on stage an uncomfortable-looking chair had been placed, though up to then no one had used it, most of the action having taken place either center-stage or on the other side. With great joy I realized that Hugh was making his way toward that chair, which stood about six or seven feet from us. Before sitting down, he stood next to it and paused, listening intently to the other players. He was so close to us I could see a faint makeup line under his chin, and as he rocked there, almost imperceptibly shifting from foot to foot and waiting to speak his next lines, I stared into his face for all I was worth.

Thinking back, it was a terrible thing to do, for as everyone knows if you stare at a person long enough, no matter what the circumstances, he's almost bound to look back at you—but I didn't think of that then. I only thought, he'll never be this close again, and then suddenly he was looking into my eyes. Our eyes had absolutely locked. His eyes had gone outside the play, outside the make-believe, and were staring back into mine with a ferocity that sent a sickening bolt of fear from the top of my head to somewhere in my gut. Actual chills radiated from my spine, and sweat literally burst out in my armpits. My stomach clenched painfully. I felt as though I'd been shot; I was terrified, but I couldn't take my eyes away. He looked almost angry—angry, I suppose, that someone had interrupted the flow of the play for him—but he kept on staring nonetheless. And then finally, after what seemed like five minutes but was probably less than one (try staring into someone's eyes for a full sixty seconds—it's a century), he broke his eyes away and spoke his next lines, and I looked down at my hands and breathed for the first time in all that staring. As soon as our gazes unlocked, the splintering pain in my head and stomach ceased.

Hugh's next task on stage was to curl up his long, long limbs into that silly chair (it had a pine-tree green velveteen seat, I'll always remember), but he almost knocked the chair over at first try, muttering under his breath lines that were certainly not in the script. I had upset his balance. He did not know who I was, but I had upset his balance.

4. Leon

Hugh thinks I'm simple. No, he's really much too smart to think that, but he needs to pretend that I'm uncomplicated enough, selfless enough, to serve him wholeheartedly as wife, mother, secretary, valet, and occasional confidante. Serve him wholeheartedly I do; selfless I am not. It's just that I love him. He pays me a great deal of money for these services as well, so I can't complain on any score. But I am not simple. No simple soul could stand to stay around Hugh Sheenan.

Hugh doesn't fool me—never has. I met him in the navy, where he was making a terrible mess of things. He tells people that it was while we were in the navy that he snatched me from the clutches of a lovely young maiden in Delhi, but that is a slight embroidery of the truth. Had he not snatched me away from her, I would have extricated myself quite soon. The woman was not worthy of either of us. Hugh and I are nearly the same age, though now of course he looks quite a bit older, and I was drawn to him at first the way many of us in the company were:

drawn to his physical radiance, his wit, his intelligence, his clownish disregard for royal rules and rigmarole, his boozing, his womanizing, and his booming Irish voice. Like me, Hugh came from quite a poor family (his Irish, mine English), and while I had educated myself as best I could and managed to improve my vocabulary and accent to a tolerable degree, I knew I could never make as grand a piece of work out of it all as he had, and I more than admired him for what he'd done.

Hugh was a young actor on the very brink of fame in those days (he'd already met with some success on the stage before joining the navy), but it wasn't the promise of glory that drew people to him; perhaps more than anything else it was his eyes. His eyes were—still are—impossible to resist. They are X-ray eyes, a true and explosive black, but one could not call them exactly beautiful. They frighten, they seduce, they command attention. And they convey highly complicated worlds. What they do more than anything else is examine. Hugh's eyes will dangle you over a stream as if you are a kitten, and then either drop you mercilessly or gather you in. Once in, in you stay. Once in, you are his, but more than that, he is yours, and you have made him vulnerable.

I had been among Hugh's ever-broadening circle of friends in the navy for some time when he finally gathered me in. I should explain that neither of us ever made it to sea in that navy (we did go to India that once, but our stay there was truncated by a threatening epidemic of an exotic fever); it was just past wartime, and neither of us was seagoing material. So we found ourselves enslaved in the Office of Personnel and Domestic Affairs—or Piss and Vinegar, as we called it—with various important and boring tasks to perform in the service of our Queen. We were, fortunately, virtually unsupervised; what supervisors we did have were too far sunk in their own quicksand of paperwork to give us much trouble.

Our collective habit (there were six of us in that sweaty pen, from six in the morning to six at night, six days a week) was to bully our way through mountains of paperwork at top speed until lunch, then make whatever plan was necessary to pull things into order for the next day and head for the pub. We'd always leave one man in charge, for emergency's sake, but once at The Dragon's Tail we'd forget whoever it was in an hour, though each of us honestly intended to go back and check on the poor bastard before day's end.

Popular as he was, Hugh rarely had to spend an afternoon at Piss and Vinegar—everyone wanted him at the pub—but every now and then, his natural sense of fair play coming forward, he'd volunteer to stay. I always wondered what he did there alone on those days. Though I knew him fairly well, I didn't really know him, and I imagined him capable of anything. I usually fancied him at his desk with a liberal supply of Galoises, a huge mug of steaming, rum-laced tea, and Miss Haverstock, the curvaceous company secretary, on his lap.

As it happened, I couldn't have been more mistaken. We sailor-boys left Hugh in charge one sweltering July afternoon and were jollying our way through our third round of bitters when I discovered I'd left my billfold in the office. I trotted on back to retrieve it, and as I neared the office door I suddenly remembered that Hugh would be there, and that this was my chance to surprise him at whatever clever or lazy or lascivious thing he was up to. I crept in through a rear door and peered around some cabinets behind Hugh's desk. I could see his endless legs stretched out in the aisle, and the room was filled with smoke and the odors of sweat and mimeograph ink, but Hugh was not engaged in any activity at all, clever or otherwise. He was leaning full back in his chair, with his great long-jawed head resting on a bookcase behind him, his hands clasped on his stomach, and his eyes closed. He was perfectly still, and I thought, of course, that he was sleeping.

Being a young fool, of course I decided to wake him up in some humiliating way. I left my hiding place and stealthily seated myself in a chair across the room from where he lay sprawled. I sat there some minutes, and was just narrowing down my choice of wake-up alarms when Hugh's voice rasped out of his mouth like a bullwhip: "What in the bloody HELL do you WANT from me, Leon?" he said.

I bolted upright, standing at full attention, like the full idiot I was. "Hugh," I said shakily. "I'm sorry, old man, I thought you were asleep."

He had not moved, or opened his eyes, and as I stood there I noticed something I could barely believe: Hugh Sheenan was weeping. Great, slow tears were running from the corners of his eyes, and with his head still thrown back they ran only the short distance into his hair, which was why at first I had not seen them. The back of his neck and his collar were sopping wet; he must have been crying for some time.

At this sight my shock evaporated, and I was naturally concerned.

"What's wrong?" I asked him. "A death in the family? Can I help?"

Slowly he sat up, still more slowly he opened his eyes. He took a large handkerchief from his pocket and unabashedly wiped his eyes, his temples, and his throat of tears. He blew his nose, loudly. He then threw the handkerchief into the dustbin. "Always preferred paper hankies," he said, and smiled. He had focused his eyes on me by this time, and though I was conscious of their fearful scrutiny, such was my concern at this oddest of occurrences that it barely affected me.

"Please," I said, "I mean, I'm sorry, old man, didn't mean to startle you, but . . ."

Hugh waved his hand magnanimously. "Think nothing of it, Leon, dear fellow. This is a public room, is it not? Your very office, indeed, is it not? The middle of a working day as well. Why shouldn't you be here? It's I who should be apologizing. I believe I've made a scene."He pulled at his tie, loosening it, and leaned back again in his chair. The telephone was ringing, but neither of us paid it any mind. He reached out his hand and I gave him my own handkerchief, upon which he honked his nose again before tossing it. "I have been weeping," he went on, "for my sins, Leon, my sins." Then he laughed a wonderful, deep-throated laugh and I joined him, though I had no idea why we were laughing.

Therein arose a long silence. Hugh was obviously not at all embarrassed by his tears; indeed, he seemed to have forgotten all about them. He smoked, and continued to examine me, not precisely in a rude manner, but in a, well, entitled one. I was not uncomfortable, but I was sorely perplexed. I wanted desperately to know what had instigated his crying jag, yet I had no idea how to find out. Was he waiting for me to start questioning him? I thought not. I could not imagine, in fact, his greeting any query of mine with anything but amazement and ridicule, and even if he deigned to answer me, I had a feeling he would not tell the truth. I thought of leaving, but it seemed out of the question; I felt I was supposed to stay. There was nothing to do but wait. I waited.

By this time, it was long past business hours, but the telephone continued to ring intermittently and we continued to ignore it. Finally, I could stand the inactivity no longer. When the phone rang again I picked it up: "Personnel and Domestic," I said in a long-unused voice that squeaked a bit. From the telephone came a male voice, nothing special about it, asking for Hugh. "I'm sorry," I said, "Mr. Sheenan has gone for the day. May I take a message?" The man said no, thank you very much, and rang off. I replaced the receiver and looked at Hugh. "For you," I told him.

He was smiling like a child, a wide, unfettered smile. He has a roomy mouth. "And did the party leave a name?"

"No name. Nothing."

"What time is it?"

"Seven thirteen," I said, looking at the huge clock that hung above us.

"Ahhh," said Hugh. "Why did you say I wasn't here?"

There was a good question. "I can't say, Hugh," I answered. "It was just a feeling."

"A marvelous feeling, Leon! A bull's-eye-centered feeling; an inspired feeling; a scrumptious, serendipitous, scalawag feeling; a feeling worth more than gold to me, old boy, and I thank you, thank you!" Hugh rose from his chair and strode over to me. He put his long, strong arms around me and hugged. He laughed and laughed. He lifted me off the floor as I stood, swung me around in a circle, and carried me to the window. It was a gesture so odd, so un-English, so unexpected, that I could not respond. I was like a doll embraced too roughly by a three-year-old.

We stood there at the window, looking out on the steel-blue Thames. Hugh kept hold of me with one arm (perhaps he was afraid I'd keel over from shock) and gestured grandly with the other. "All of this, Leon my boy," he said, shaking me. "All of this and much, much more will be ours. We'll travel together, we'll conquer worlds. I think I can make a little money, Leon, and we shall be comfortable and famous and grow old among lovely women and drink rare wines and wear white jackets. And Leon, we shall sing, and recite the great poems, and waltz and waltz our days away."

At that he released me and began to dance around the room, crooning a three-four melody in some enchanted language of his own, snatching up an overcoat along the way and waltzing with it tenderly, as if it were a princess. I thought his singing voice was pleasant.

I had turned to stone, and yet my heart was pounding. I did not know exactly what he was proposing, or whether he was drunk or drugged (or, it crossed my mind, perhaps even homosexual), or even if he meant a word of what he'd said, but I knew I'd been gathered in.I felt sincerely good. I watched Hugh dance around for a time until at last he alighted on a desk near the door.

"To the streets!" he commanded.

We went out and drank hard all night, and helped each other home toward dawn. At no point did the secrets of his afternoon tears or the mysterious telephone caller reveal themselves, but it did not matter. I knew Hugh would always have secrets from me.

We worked side by side in Piss and Vinegar until we were joyfully discharged a year later, never again going out alone together in all that time. And yet I did not question our understanding. On the day we took off our uniforms for the last time, Hugh came to my room. He stood in the doorway and looked at me for some minutes.

He smiled the child's smile again at last. "I'm off to the country for a spell, to the soothing hills of Ireland," he told me. "To . . . undigest . . . all this. I wish you would come."

And I did of course, and we've been together ever since.

5. Rick

When I first saw Nora I was looking for a job. She was working in a bookstore in Boston and I had applied for a part-time position there while I was finishing grad school. She was the strangest thing; I wanted immediately to kiss her. She was all wispy hair and angles and funny eyes, and her knit blouse clung to her small breasts like the icing on cupcakes. Later, after we'd become lovers, she told me she'd fallen for me that day too, so I guess it was really love at first sight, just the way people describe it.

I got the job. We saw each other every day for four months, both at work and after, then moved in together. The fourth year we broke up. The fifth year we got married. So all in all we've known each other nine years, which seems incredible. I can't imagine life without Nora, though I do sometimes. I guess she thinks about life without me too, but I know neither of us wants to be apart. She's a pisser, though, to be truthful. A real pisser.

The thing about her is, she's a dreamer. She has this unstoppable imagination and she lives in it much of the time. I don't mean she's spaced out. On the contrary, if you asked any of her friends to name the most responsible, practical person they know, they would say Nora. She's successful in her job and in almost everything she tries, but she's never really happy about it. She's cheerful, she's positive, but she's a positive pessimist, if you know what I mean. She keeps on going, but she isn't sure why. What she sees in me is a mystery, but I'm glad she sees it. She sort of holds me together, and I guess I give her a kind of anchor in her life of dreams.

Nora enjoys her heroes more than most people; she seems to almost "know" them personally, she takes such an interest in them. I can only think of a few just now, and in no particular order: Jane Goodall, Oscar Wilde, David Bowie, Edith Wharton, a radio talk-show host named Jerry Williams, Kevin McHale of the Celtics, her college psychology professor, and that actor Hugh Sheenan. There are others too, but I think I've hit the main ones. Hugh Sheenan occupied her spotlight recently when she went to see him in a play in New York City. She came home that night slightly dazed and glassy-eyed and . . . quiet. The way she acted made me wish I'd gone with her, but I didn't think much about it. I like the guy too, but I'd had other plans that weekend. She was behaving oddly, but I was glad she'd had a good time.

6. Nora

We went to dinner after the play, at a Japanese restaurant full of happy-looking people, a very nice place. I made a big show of trying to find out who had won the Celtics game that afternoon, but of course we were in New York, not Boston, so I didn't have much luck. Here and there my sister and I were able to exchange a few sensible words. My mother was happy with her appetizer of crabsticks in a seaweed cone. The whole time I wondered what I was doing with these people; or, to be more precise, I wondered if I really *was* with these people. My body was, certainly; it had just downed, in speedy fashion, a huge, sizzling meal and two beers. But I felt ridiculously like someone who had just been to Lourdes and seen the Virgin: calm and blessed, with a heart full of secrets and visions no one would ever believe.

I sat in the back seat of Belinda's car on the way home and pretended to sleep so no one would bother me. The air-conditioning lulled me, and the conversation and music from the tape deck seemed as far away as Mars. My mind circled endlessly around the last few minutes of the play, the minutes when Hugh had, as I thought of it, touched me. Something had certainly happened, something privileged and intangible, but I could not put a name to it—I guess I was still too "shocky." I wondered how long it had taken Hugh to forget the incident; I had no doubt that it had affected him too but imagined, reasonably, that he had other fish to fry and would pass it off as a momentary annoyance, albeit an unnerving one. Also, I had more than an inkling that this sort of thing probably happened all the time. I wasn't really special; I just felt that way.

By the time Belinda dropped us off at my mother's it was quite late, but I felt I had to call Rick. I hadn't talked to him since the morning I left, and I was anxious to hear his voice. I wanted to tell him about the play, but, more than that, I think I hoped his voice would bring me down to earth a little. I have always been a little scared of heights.

When I say it was quite late I mean it was probably around eleven. Rick is a night owl; I had no fear of waking him. In fact, I thought he'd be waiting for my call. But although he was nice as pie, it was as if I'd only been gone an hour. We talked for a couple of minutes, he inquired about everyone and told me about his day, but he never asked me about *The Lion's Share*. I couldn't believe it. I finally said, "Aren't you going to ask me if I had a good time in the city?"

"Of course," he said. "I was just going to. How was it?"

So I told him it was great and gave a few details to be polite, and we signed off in our usual way, with *I love yous* on both sides. I was slightly pissed. I thought he hadn't inquired about the play on purpose; after all, *The Lion's Share* had been the whole reason for my trip. Before I left for my mother's he'd teased me about Hugh, seeming to take it all in spirit of good fun. And hadn't I put up with all sorts of little obsessions of his over the years? Was he suddenly starting to take things too seriously? It bothered me a little, but I must confess it didn't bother me long. I went right to bed. I hoped I would dream of Hugh, but whether I did or not I can't recall. I slept deeply and the next morning I was eager to be on my way and greedily alone with my thoughts, like a child intent on being alone with a bag of candy.

It was a perfect day to drive four hours: partly cloudy, on the cool side, and not too many people on the road. I felt as if I could drive forever, and though I kept the radio on to check out the talk shows in the states I passed through, I hardly heard a thing. I relived the play, going over all the lines I could remember and vividly picturing the cast as they spoke them—especially Hugh, of course. Partly I did this for the sheer pleasure of it, but mostly I did it to keep that afternoon alive in my mind by cutting its groove in my memory deeper and deeper. I knew if I "practiced" I had a better chance of keeping things clear.

Then, when I was about an hour from Boston, I allowed myself to take out the best, which I'd been saving hungrily for last. I could still call up that sickly "shot" feeling just by thinking about my eyes and Hugh's fastening upon each other outside of time—for that was what our "encounter" seemed to have been. I pictured the scene as if it were a painting or drawing executed from a vantage point in the rear of the theater: the audience in near darkness, the stage and the players alive in light, and Hugh standing off to the left of the set, looking down into the audience with a startled, incredulous gaze. I thought of it as the kind of old-fashioned picture you might see illustrating a Wilkie Collins novel: millions of tiny, finely etched lines, people's gesticulations frozen as if they were playing a game of statues, and ardent shafts of light illuminating the vital centers of action. One of these shafts of light went directly from Hugh to me.

And then I pictured it from other angles, close in and far off, and even from the stage. I tried to see myself from Hugh's eyes, sitting there with my pale dress and my ceaseless stare, but I couldn't really imagine my face: the strange, ageless woman I'd seen in the bathroom was always sitting in my seat.

Lastly, when I had led myself slowly up to this final delight, I played back the moments Hugh looked at me, and each time I shivered with the wonder of it. Like making love, it left me feeling both strong and lightheaded.

When I was weak from remembering, I tried to examine a small, gnawing feeling of dissatisfaction that had cropped up along the way, and I realized that I felt guilty; I had received so much that Sunday afternoon, and I had returned not a thing to the giver.

I knew this was absurd, but I had been a guilt-freak from childhood. Once, for example, we were given a wonderful treat in school (it couldn't have been later than second grade): we were allowed to see a film in the auditorium in the middle of the day, a film purely for pleasure, unrelated to any studies, and as I sat there, I was entranced and excited, yes, but I also couldn't erase from my mind the feeling that the experience would only be perfect if my mother and father, who worked so hard all day, could be there too. Perhaps this is an experience common to children, but I've never heard anyone else confess such a memory, and I have always attributed this syndrome to a neurotic inability to enjoy myself for my own sake.

At any rate, it was then I decided to write a letter. At first I thought a simple thank-you to Hugh would do, but then I tried to think of something I could send him. Naturally I knew this was no original idea: a star of his brilliance must receive oceans of fan mail, all sorts of gifts. I also knew the chances of his ever seeing my own humble missive were remote, but I had to try. What could I send him? A book, perhaps? A box of home-baked cookies? Ha.

Everything I thought of seemed fantastically stupid, and for the first time on that blissful drive I began to get annoyed. I could send him a pair of gloves (he always wore pale blue ones, no matter what the season—some kind of lucky symbol for him), but that seemed presumptuously personal and not even original. I imagined a storeroom somewhere in his house full of boxes of blue gloves fans had sent him. There was nothing for it; I simply couldn't think. And anyway, by that time I was heading into the underpass on Huntington Avenue. It was time to face reality, and Rick.

7. Hugh

As I said, in those days I was a man in a trance. Life was going nicely, but I hardly heeded it. For once, I lived quietly, and was given to long, leisurely walks in Central Park (Leon trailing a discreet half-block behind), where I would give myself over to the contemplation of pigeons, leaves, and the avoidance of dog poop on the paths. For several days I seriously considered trying to market a special type of comfortable walking shoe my imagination had devised: shoes that felt like clouds but looked like shoes, not like the ubiquitous American footwear meant originally for leaping hurdles and running races. Nothing quite hurt my aesthetic sense as much on those walks as seeing a lovely woman in a smart summer suit with huge, rubber-boat-like tennies at the end of her shapely legs. This imaginary project held my interest for some time.

I suppose I was fortunate I had nothing more serious to worry me. Even my health was on the upswing, physically at least. Leon had not felt the need to dose me in weeks, and I was often sleeping more than four hours a night and waking more or less rested. I amused myself with the notion that I was "re-growing" my heart. My long walks had refreshed me, had taken the old, familiar, weary stiffness from my limbs, and I found this new resiliency was even making my work on stage easier: traveling from right stage to left no longer seemed like a breathless trek across the Sahara.

But the morning after I dreamed of that odd young woman I did not feel rested at all. I did not get out of bed until noon, and I felt cranky enough to call Leon to task for forgetting to take a spot out of my new linen suit. Leon in turn felt insulted enough (after all, I had at least four identical linen suits) to revenge himself by offering me coffee. I was happy to drink it; I felt I needed to be punished for the dream, and while the coffee did not wreak its usual vengeance on my innards, it did accelerate my metabolism to a truly frightening degree. My pulse was pattering madly.

I was dressed in a flash, and though the matinee was more than two hours off, I made haste for the theater. I did not take the blue car, and I did not take Leon. I walked. And I was not in disguise. I walked down Sixth Avenue that May afternoon with my foolish head held high and the most arrogant expression on my face that I could muster. That is to say, I felt exceedingly bold, and I sailed along at top speed with my trench coat flapping and my arms swinging like twin scythes. Several people stopped dead in their tracks, but none dared approach me.

I walked so quickly, in fact, that upon reaching the theater, I suddenly realized I'd arrived far too soon, and I turned briskly into the first tavern I saw that did not have those tiny high windows set into a blank facade. Americans are so ashamed of their drinking that they board up many of their public houses so no one can see inside. Ridiculous, hypocritical, unhealthy habit. I chose a place with plate glass windows and lots of white furniture visible from the street, sat at a comfortable table in the rear, and ordered a double whiskey. I knew I could not drink it, but the very size of the thing would afford me time to brood. The waiter asked me for my autograph and I obliged, signing the name of another actor (of whom I was often jealous)—but he, poor, star-stricken dolt, was too befuddled to notice. I asked for a glass of water, drank half, poured a thimbleful of whiskey into the tumbler, positioned my Galoises and lighter for easy access, and sat back to think.

What was this feeling that bloody dream had produced in me? I had never put much stock in dreams, but I had to admit this one was bothering me mightily. I had not wanted it to be over—that accounted for my grisly mood upon wakening—and I felt at that moment that if I could be assured I'd enter that particular dream again, I would lay my head down on the table in that bar and give up that day's performance or anything else. Some of the details had become fuzzy, but I could call up the pull of that young woman's eyes at will, and the feeling it gave me was at once a puzzle and a comfort. Was she someone I actually knew, but had forgotten? Was she merely the creation of my addled old brain? Or, worst of all, was she the embodiment of all the comfort my soul now desired but would never find?

That was it. I knew it. The small solace dreaming that dream had bestowed upon me was dashed; I was convinced all at once I was doomed to live the rest of my besotted life like a man who could never obtain the one thing he wanted: silent—and instant—understanding. It was worse than simple loneliness, closer to despair.

And a fat load of rubbish, I did realize. I told myself I was merely having a belated reaction to my more or less recent divorce, and that it was only natural that I would have to face the music sooner or later. It had been my second marriage. My first, embarked upon rather early in youth, had endured over twenty years, and although its ending had been difficult and sad, I remained on excellent terms with my first wife, and time had long since mellowed regret to a comfortable wisdom. When that first marriage was over, I had immersed myself in my work for a number of years, and traveled the world over, picking up the most fantastic women here and there but never staying with any of them very long. There had been scores of them. I say this not boastfully, but with gratitude. They were beautiful, they were sexually all I could desire, and they had, for the most part, been terribly kind to me. For if, those days in New York, I was a man in a trance, in the days after my first marriage dissolved I was a man intent on hell. I could feel a sick brilliance within me breaking the surface of my skin like some terrible itching disease, and I drank and womanized and worked like a bloody bastard at a string of exhausting (and not terribly successful) theatrical projects and film roles.

I also spent money prodigally, and Leon was forced at last to shelve his own salary for a period of some months. That and that alone shook me to reform; I could not bear his silent charity. So Leon and I returned to England: I with my headaches, heartaches, stomachaches, and guilt, and he with an admirable attitude of relief and concern. We set about restoring my life to some kind of order. I sold several cars, accepted a script for a promising American movie, and eschewed many pleasures I was used to absorbing mindlessly and daily. It was then my doctors discovered the deplorable state of my heart. A lengthy operation and three dreadful weeks in hospital furthered my reclamation, and I returned to the London house (which fortunately I'd managed to keep) to recuperate, a changed fellow.

Leon nursed me, cursed me, and kept the public at bay. I remained essentially housebound for nearly two years—by choice, not by doctors' direction. I meditated on my childhood in Ireland, where I'd spent my early years. I reflected, for the first time in eons, upon my parents' accidental double death. I mourned for them with a child's simple grief; its intensity stunned me, and I turned for a time into what Leon refers to as "the wild child." I considered, in fact, my entire youth, including my Canadian years, when I'd been cared for by my good aunt Kate, a kindly, deeply religious woman and a ceaseless knitter of pretty blue gloves, which she called, for some apocryphal reason I can' t remember, "St. Patty's mittens." I was encouraged to wear them everywhere but to bed.

When I turned eighteen, Aunt Kate allowed me, with tears in her sparkling Irish eyes, to remake my Atlantic crossing, where at last I encountered, in London, the reason for my life: The Stage. It was odd how completely my memory had previously forsaken my Vancouver days; at most they had always called to mind the rainy, windless weather I'd always loved—that I still love in England.

And, too, I read poetry, sitting for hours in the whirlpool Leon had had installed and sprawling on a sand-chair in all weathers on my front lawn with a glass of what Leon called "faux gin" (Perrier) by my side. I was befriended by a stripy stray tomcat whom I dubbed Horatio; he would sit forever on a rug at my feet but would rarely allow me to touch him. I imagined myself saying to him, ". . . There are more things in heaven and earth, Horatio, than are dreamt of in your philosophy."

The day I realized I was considering writing my memoirs was the day I knew I had to get out of the house. So I accepted another American script—I had almost been forgotten by this point, but not quite—Leon packed our trunks, and we set off again across the seas.

Women were out of the question: not only did my physical debilitation make the idea of sex strangely repugnant to me (I had the expected fear of dropping dead in an unworthy hussy's arms and being discovered in some humiliating position—a fear I gradually, thank God, outgrew), but I had also found a certain peace in my recuperative years that was made up mostly of avoidance. Of course there were lonely days and nights, but I was so dreadfully tired.

In America I met Maryann, though I did not meet her immediately. Leon had found a pleasant rental in the hills outside Los Angeles and we sculpted a quiet life there, as quiet a life as being in films permits. I did go out to parties and such, perhaps once a week, but I never asked anyone home. While out, I considered my old image worth reviving, and would down vast quantities of faux gin—pretending, of course, that it *was* gin, and acting it up accordingly.

This made me both popular and worth avoiding simultaneously, since the new regime in Hollywood, although dopers and profligates for the most part, were riding the crest of the "clean living" wave, and flamboyant alcoholics were only just tolerated by the younger crowd. Maryann was the sister of one of these younger actors, and I was introduced to her some months after my arrival at a gallery opening where the actor's simplistic photographs were being exhibited. She was perhaps ten years my junior, but about her was a pure and old-fashioned air that attracted me at once. Physically, she looked like an English "mod," which was also, by that time, old-fashioned, and this outmodedness touched my heart in a well-callused place. I did not find these stirrings distasteful.

I think now that poor Maryann allowed herself to be swept away more by my image than by my person. I suppose I had grown tired of myself during my long seclusion, and when we began keeping company I allowed her to feel too soon that my intentions were serious. She took the outcome of our affair as predestined from that time on, but I did not notice at first that this attitude was taking a lot of the fun out of things. I courted her like a storybook knight, and it did not take long to win my prize.

Leon was astonished the first time I brought her home.

"An American girl?" he asked the next morning, attempting to seem casual.

"Yes, Leon," I said. "But try not to hold it against her. She comes from the East; she is not one of these loon-brained California maidens you so despise, and I happen to admire her a great deal, so you will be seeing more of her."

"Then I will not need to have a messenger return these?" Leon asked, holding up a pair of long-legged silver hose. I gazed at him. His face crinkled. And together, we began to laugh a laugh that had been too long under the earth.

"Like old times, Hugh," said Leon. "Like the good old times."

But after Maryann and I were married it was not like old times. Not at all. It was nothing like my first marriage. My first wife was a highly intelligent woman, a passionate woman, and very much her own person; never could she have survived so many years in my company had she been anything else. Had I been faithful to her? "In my fashion," I had been, and she'd understood that. And she to me? I do not know, or care to.

I am sure Maryann never even considered such things; they would have been beyond her ken. She had no power to reason further than the conventional.

Maryann was not brainless, but she was guileless, and I found it hard to distinguish between the two. Her old-fashioned air, I discovered, included a rather stodgy worldview, one in which no oddity of life, no human peculiarity, could be heralded as interesting, much less accepted as a bonus to quotidian existence. She focused herself on me and my activities in a way I found made me profoundly paranoid. I also grew tired of her in bed, where she was the queen of clinging vines, and became daily more disgusted with myself for having fallen prey to a simple loneliness I had not properly identified at the time. I had fancied myself in love with her, when it was only age and vanity—tempered, of course, by affection.

I continued to treat Maryann nicely (if insincerity can be called "nice"), and to sleep with her when it was unavoidable, and she for her part continued to put up with me for lack of the ability to invent a good reason to leave. I know my growing dissatisfaction must have hurt her, though I tried to cover it as best I could. By the time I was quite fed up (it only took a month or so), Maryann was with child, and that improved things for a time. I had no heir from my previous marriage and I wanted one. Maryann was devoted to me, if boring, and I felt I could live with her and the child if I watched my manners and conducted my personal life in a way that could damage neither of them. I did not wish for other women in this secret life I imagined; I envisioned only the stuporous contentment of waking alone and looking for some kind of new inspiration in each day.

A little girl was born to us just before our first anniversary, and we called her Ruby. Or I should say I called her Ruby, for in a rare fit of assertiveness Maryann had insisted on formally naming her Raychelle, after her grandmother. I considered Raychelle Sheenan an intolerable appellation, but I did not argue. I simply addressed the baby as Ruby, and Ruby she quickly became, to one and all. This so infuriated Maryann that she made life at last visibly miserable enough for us to separate. One would not think such a thing could occasion a marital rift, but indeed it did: the fruit of our incompatibility was ripe to burst.

When Ruby was two, Maryann took her east to her family, and my long-confused and hidden heart was broken. I had meant to see the child every weekend, but distance and work (which was fortunately in good supply) made this often impossible, and my darling girl-child began to seem no more than a piquant memory. I did see her, however, perhaps every month or so, and Ruby grew only more precious to me for her infrequent availability. She called me "Papa-man," and seemed fond enough of me in her distracted child's way. Maryann and I had entered upon no legal separation, but toward the time when we might have been celebrating four years of marital bliss, she suddenly divorced me. She had found someone else, as was inevitable, and while she assured me she had no actual plans to give Ruby a step-papa-man, she also told me she was finding the infinite extension of our sham marriage too bleak a condition to bear. I could not blame her. My solicitors allowed her a generous settlement, and I would be able to see Ruby whenever it seemed reasonable to all concerned. Very civilized.

And though I craved the company of my daughter, I could see no reason to dally any longer in the States. In four years, Leon and I had returned to England only twice, for very short visits, and I was aching for my comfortable, empty home and its familiar consolations. I even began to wonder if my funny cat Horatio still remembered me ("Art thou there, truepenny?") And I told Leon that as soon as we could, we would go to Ireland for a time, where I hoped the fragrant air of my ancestors would restore to me some lost greatness.

When I looked at last at my watch it was time, nearly past time, to make for the theater. Guilt-stricken by my lengthy musings, I left my poor devil of a waiter a monumental tip. Leon greeted me at the stage door with a murderous look, hauled me inside roughly, and stood me up like a doll against my dressing-room door.

"It's god-awful, Hugh, the way you worried us!" he said. "You ought to be paddled and locked in your room for a week, you great, stupid child!" His bulldoggy face was red and white with anger, the whites of his eyes were shot with crimson, and his voice cracked as he scolded me. Under stress, what I heartlessly called Leon's "working-class face" always sprang into prominence; he looked like a gargoyle straining to leap from its cathedral. "You have about five minutes to dress," he said, "so get on with it, man, and we'll talk about all this later."

I tried to catch hold of him and calm him down, but he was out of the room before I could move, and I felt truly sorry. "You are a fucking-bloody-selfish-hopeless idiot," I told myself, and vowed that I would make it up to Leon somehow and reform my dreadful habits for a week or two at least.

Then it hit me that perhaps Leon was in need of a vacation. As far as I could remember, except for a few fleeting visits to his family now and then, he had barely left my side for many years. I never found Leon's presence intrusive, but then, no matter how rooted in friendship were our daily working relations, I was still in truth "the boss," and when I needed to be free of Leon I simply commanded him to be gone. He, on the other hand, had access to no such relief, and since mine was the far more difficult and abrasive personality, I told myself Leon must have his rest; I would send him off on an enforced leave, for a period of time not less than a month, for purposes of rest and reconstitution.

I decided to "lay it on him," as the Americans so aptly say, right after the matinee. I would miss him sorely, but I would just have to get by.

Cheered by this heroically selfless decision, I played well that afternoon. My voice was strong, my timing tip-top, and my confidence so overwhelming, even to me, that my only struggle was keeping myself in check. The house was packed; there were even standees in the rear (I had peeked out like an ingénue from behind the curtain before it rose), and there was in the air that indefinable crackling of acceptance that keeps a performer's heart thumping with excitement no matter how many times he's spoken his lines.

At intermission the place was abuzz, and backstage even Leon was smiling, though he succeeded in never smiling once at me. *It's all right*, I thought, *I shall straighten the dear boy out when this is over.* So when, toward the end of the last act, I lost my mental footing for a moment, I was most unpleasantly surprised.

It wasn't that I'd forgotten my lines; indeed, I was not even supposed to be speaking when it happened. I had moved, as planned, slowly from one side of the stage to the other, listening to the ongoing dialogue, and was standing very close to the front of the platform, looking out into nothingness, waiting for my turn to speak. My only task at this point in the play was to look bemused. Usually, this pause in the action gave me welcome relief, since my speaking parts were long and fairly constant throughout, but that day as I stood there I began to feel nervous and frightened. I can only say that I felt somehow besieged, and the attack, or whatever it was, was definitely coming from outside the play, not from the actors behind me. It flashed through my mind that perhaps there was something monstrous happening in the theater, that perchance a lunatic was loose in the mezzanine or a fire had been instigated from someone's outlaw cigar.

But I knew instantly there was no public danger. The threat was centered on me.

I battled with all my considerable stage experience not to "leave" the play, but I was in the grip of a panic greater than any actor's determination. So I did the unthinkable: I looked down, down from the nothingness on which I had hung all my attention, and down into the first few rows of seats, a scant seven feet or so beneath me.

From the first row a woman was staring into my eyes. I am sure this had happened before, many times—one can hardly have played on so many stages without occasionally catching the determined eye of an audience member—but this was somehow outlandish. Our eyes caught hold and locked; there's no other way to state it. I was furious with her for having disturbed my concentration, and I hoped my face was showing her some of that fury (while still retaining my character's proper façade of course), but *I could not take my eyes from hers.* I barely saw the rest of her such was the vise my view was held in, but I had a vague impression of a yellowness of dress and a lightness of hair. I also knew, though I barely saw, that her mouth was a little open and slightly smiling.

This woman and I carried on our private, illicit exchange for some minutes, or what couldn't have been, but seemed like, some minutes, during which neither of us blinked. Horrendous.

At last I was able to look away, my ears at least having had enough sense to listen independently for my cue, and my lips to speak my next line—thank God in heaven a short one. I was then to walk toward a chair near the edge of the set and curl up into it, but when I attempted this familiar feat I nearly missed my mark, executing a clumsy motion that almost tipped the chair, and then banging my bones into the seat so that the impact must have been felt in the last rows of the theater. I muttered some bugger-it-alls and went on with my lines, ignoring a few titters I heard from the audience. I knew they would forgive me almost anything, and would even feel privileged to have witnessed this little gaucheness, but I was still furious—with myself, with the chair, and with that brazen little baggage in the first row.

She had somehow managed to hurt me, and I would never be able to tell her so.

8. Rick

I forgot to mention Nora's art, which is strange since it's one of the things that drew me to her in the first place. She was artistic in almost every way, "different," that is to say—in her hairstyle and dress, and in almost all her tastes—but she could also blend into just about any group. It was an attractive quality.

I watched her closely at the bookstore for about a week before I asked her out the first time, and in those few days I saw about six or seven different Noras, all of them true to herself, but each of them showing that ultimate charity of making everyone she spoke with feel comfortable. She could talk to the janitor or the boss or a college student or an old lady and find some common ground with each of them. She was quiet about it; I don't think too many of our coworkers noticed how good she was with people. In fact, I think the general consensus was that Nora was shy. But I noticed, and I liked her for it. And the funny thing was that it didn't really gel with her eternal pessimism, or even her dreaminess, but there you are. She's "complicated."

Anyway, one day, about two weeks into our relationship, Nora invited me home for dinner. She lived in an attic apartment in one of the suburbs, which she had furnished sparely, but with comfort and individuality. There were some funny little drawings tacked up over her desk and hung about the place in cheap, colorful frames. They were scratchy, black-and-white things, with an occasional burst of color that lent them a certain whimsical tone. One in particular caught my eye: a drawing, about a foot square, of an overcrowded, weedy garden, full of trowels and rakes and such, and in one corner a little turquoise-blue rose, more carefully drawn than the other flowers, with a yellowish sort of halo around it containing a bright red bee. I don't know why I liked it so much, but I really did, and I asked her about it. "I did that last summer," she said, "when I was visiting my aunt." And then, very seriously, as if she were letting me in on an important secret, "There really aren't any roses that color, you know."

I liked that, and I was thrilled and surprised that Nora had made the pictures. Thinking back, I guess it never occurred to me that she was the artist because, for one thing, in the two weeks I'd known her she'd never spoken about her drawing, and for another, there was absolutely no sign of paper, paint, crayons, or anything else of an artsy nature visible in her apartment. She had everything hidden away. I told her I was impressed, especially with the bee picture, and she seemed to like that, but we didn't talk about it very long.

I gradually learned that her art was like her dreaming: something she needed terribly and held dear, but wanted to keep essentially private. She'd show me things now and then of course, and once in a while, in a romantic moment, would dream aloud that we lived together and were rich and she could stop working at the bookstore and draw all day, but it wasn't a frequent topic. And sometimes she'd send a picture to a magazine and they'd like it and print it next to a short story or something, and pay her a little money. I knew that made her really proud. One of the great regrets of my life is that for our first anniversary Nora gave me the picture of the rose and the bee, and I, great dolt that I am, managed somehow to lose it when we moved to a new apartment. It hurt her feelings, I know, though she never held it against me.

Well, I hadn't seen too many of Nora's little pictures in a while when I discovered a really fine one accidentally, while searching for some stationery in her room. (We had a bedroom together, of course, but we both had a tiny hide-away room of our own; that was one thing Nora insisted upon, and I loved it too. Staying apart that way made our time together more special. Nora called her room "Virginia's room" after *A Room of One's Own*.) I remember clearly that it was the week after that trip to New York when she went to the play with her mother, because I was looking for the stationery to write to an employer about a new job I was after, and I got the job—so I remember the date. I found the paper where I expected it to be (Nora was awfully neat) and then noticed what looked like a drawing turned face down on top of the bookcase.

I turned it over. It was exquisite.

It was so exquisite, in fact, it gave me kind of a shock. The picture was the same favored size of many of Nora's works—about a foot square, maybe a little smaller—and it was the usual black and white with a bit of color, but there was something hauntingly different about it that kept me standing there quite some time. I carried it over to the light to look some more. The scene showed the inside of some kind of big auditorium, the point of view somewhere high up in the balcony, off to the right. Light was dim everywhere, except around the stage, but you could make out many individual heads and hats and the shapes of the seatbacks and steps leading down to the front. On stage there were some people in costume (you couldn't tell exactly what kind, but you could see it wasn't modern-day dress), most of them gathered off to the right. And in the very front of the stage, on the left, stood a tall man in an odd posture. It was subtly odd; he appeared at first glance just to be standing there upright, but on further examination you could see that he was inclined slightly forward, and that he was looking down.

A shaft of light, colored the palest of yellows, led from the man's face to a head in one of the front rows of the audience, and when I examined the picture under the lamp on Nora's desk I saw the most remarkable expression on the face of the man, an expression of anger and wonder, and I noticed the only other color in the drawing: a vivid blue-black, used for his eyes. So tiny, and so subtle (to call attention to a particular "blackness" in a black-and-white drawing seemed quite a feat), were these dots of color that they had at first escaped my notice, but once I'd seen them they seemed to bounce uncannily off the shaft of yellow light and to give the man's face an animation that was truly delightful.

I say "delightful," but I was delighted only with the artistic value of the thing; in another way it gave me the creeps, though at the time I couldn't have explained why. Maybe that's why I didn't mention to Nora that I'd seen it when she got home that day. Maybe I was waiting for her to bring it and show it to me (then I would have had a lot of questions). But several weeks went by, weeks filled with many distractions, and neither of us ever mentioned her new drawing.

I went into her room only once again during that time, ostensibly on another innocent errand but with the firm intention of viewing that drawing again. I couldn't find it. I hoped she hadn't destroyed it; I thought she'd probably sent it to a magazine. I'd wanted to see it again, but I can't really say I was sorry it was gone.

9. Leon

We went back to London directly after Hugh's divorce from Maryann, but we never got to Ireland. I can't say I was sorry; I liked Hugh' s hideaway cottage there, its quietness and isolation, but the country of his birth seemed to bring out a brooding Hugh, and in the past I'd seen him sink into the deepest reveries and the lengthiest, most morose "downs" (as the Americans say) over what seemed to me mere trifles. The absence of his daughter, certain only to be exacerbated by distance, would almost definitely have caused him to fall into one of these depressions, and I didn't have the stomach for it, not this time.

So it was with secret glee that I greeted Hugh's announcement several weeks after we'd landed at Heathrow that he'd been offered the lead in *The Lion's Share,* which was to play a definite engagement of at least one month on Broadway, and that he was seriously considering the deal. It was a play he loved and had starred in once before, long ago, to rave reviews in the West End, but he had been much younger then and he told me he now felt he'd "grown into" the role. Also, I suspected, he was hoping that he could see quite a bit of Ruby in the States and perhaps even spirit her away from her mother for a while. . . maybe even a long while. His fervent wish was to raise the child in Europe, mother or no mother, though I didn't see how he'd pull that off, with Maryann being an exemplary parent and the child accustomed to nothing since birth but American ways.

Less than a month in London, some quick rehearsals (during which Hugh was lauded as "perfect" for his part), and we were headed again for the States. This time at least, I told myself, we wouldn't be immersed in a state of fake luxury in that awful California; New York, if dirty and dangerous, is a tad more civilized and to my taste. We set up in a nifty hotel and the play opened to surprisingly receptive American hearts. It seemed assured to run a favorable course, perhaps well into the summer.

Hugh was doing splendidly, both professionally and personally. Except for occasional bouts of gloom and doom (usually occurring after one of Ruby's weekend visits), he was sleeping and eating better and staying away from the liquor and the ladies. I rarely heard him voice a complaint or concern about his heart. (He seemed to have forgotten about his uncertain physical condition, and the doctors assured me that this was a healthy development. Since I was looking out for him, it was better for him to proceed as he normally did; I kept him from overdoing without inhibiting his activities too noticeably much. This put the strain on me, but I was willing to accept it.) He worked like a demon, never missed a performance, and even forced himself to be cooperative with the media, appearing on several late-night television shows, a practice he abhorred and usually avoided assiduously. Hugh did not come over well in an interview: he appeared wild-eyed and distracted, and laughed a good deal at nothing, but this play had endeared him to New Yorkers somehow, so that even his foolishness was lovingly accepted.

I welcomed also the return of our comradeship of old, a relation that had necessarily been weakened by his marriage and Ruby's birth, and by my own dissatisfaction with the Los Angeles locale. In New York that summer Hugh and I regressed in a delightful way. He rarely bid me to leave him, and even on his long walks in Central Park, when I tailed him some paces behind to give him his privacy, we enjoyed our familiar communion of souls.

In truth, I worried about him on these walks. What was to prevent some madman, recognizing Hugh (or even not recognizing him at all except as a well-dressed and lonely stroller), from robbing or beating or God forbid even kidnapping him right out from under my large, working-class nose? But nothing of the sort happened, naturally; we rarely encountered anyone at all. And I was cheered to see the change in Hugh for the better.

At night when he could not sleep (he still had the occasional bout of insomnia) we'd sometimes play cards, or I'd read to him, or, and this was best, Hugh would simply talk and talk. He is a man of amazing sensitivity and intelligence, and his vocabulary, and the way he used it to dramatic and often comic effect, had always thrilled me—always shall.

On one night I remember especially from our time in that posh hotel, Hugh told me about a peculiar dream he'd had a few weeks before.

It was strange the way he spoke of that dream: there was a certain reverence in his delivery that was usually reserved for the very few topics Hugh considered unworthy of the smallest scorn. (This included such themes as children—though only since he'd become a father—Ireland, the avoidance of "unnecessary" wars, and of course Acting.) And there was a certain innocence as well, a charming display of awe, tempered by a bit of what seemed like superstition. Hugh was superstitious to a degree (about his famous blue gloves, for example), but always with a touch of self-deprecation.

This time there was none of that. He lay on his back in that big brass hotel bed with his hands behind his head and the covers pulled up to his chin, and spoke to the ceiling in a low, sleepy voice that mesmerized me.

"It was the night of my birthday," he began. "Do you remember, Leon, how ill I was that night?" (Indeed I did, but he did not wait for a reply.) "When you put me to bed with that warlock's elixir of yours I felt as though I were making straight for heaven, but to heaven I did not go. I went into a dream, Leon, a strange dream that has bothered me quite a bit since then." Silence for a minute, and then, "Shall I tell it to you?"

I said, "Yes, do."

"I'd like to tell it, if telling would only help, but somehow I doubt it will," Hugh said, and heaved an exhausted sigh. He almost sounded sorry for himself, which truly surprised me.Even on his worst days, Hugh had never been one for self-pity; he was more the angry, sarcastic, hysterical sort. So I put my feet up and Hugh told me the dream. There wasn't much to it; indeed, I had been expecting something on the order of a Russian novel, in intensity if not in length. This was a simple dream, harking back to a scene in one of his last Hollywood films, in which he is sitting on the roof of a country church in the moonlight. I had always liked that part of the film; it showed off both Hugh's murkier spiritual depths and his still-powerful physical attractions to perfection. He'd dreamed, he told me, that he'd fallen off the roof, done a bit of slow-motion falling, and landed unhurt at the feet of a young woman, a stranger to him, who somehow stared him into some kind of hypnosis that was so uncomfortable it had awakened him and left him out of sorts for days.

I was about to make some inane comment (I didn't really know what to make of it all), but telling the dream seemed to have exhausted Hugh, and he fell suddenly asleep, like a huge puppy. I recalled then that it was the day after his birthday that he'd taken off on his own like a damned fool and arrived at the theater nearly late, scaring me witless.

I also remembered that it was during that particular performance that he seemed to have taken some sort of fit, a little like the petit mal of epilepsy, while he was onstage—an occurrence that both astounded and terrified me, but which, I soon learned, I seemed to have been the only one to notice. One of the stagehands had practically thrown a body-block to stop me from rushing the stage at that moment, and when that quick-thinking gentleman released me and asked me what on earth was the matter, I realized no one else had noticed anything at all amiss.

Hugh was a little clumsy that afternoon on stage as well, which also worried me, but when I questioned him later about what had happened, he inquired if I didn't think that a person who had performed the same part for "a million-million nights and days" had the right to display a bit of human frailty now and then. I had to see his point.

But he was a beast that evening, and for several ensuing days—prey to an ugly, self-destructive mood—and I became not just exasperated but more worried than ever about his health. No matter what anyone else said, I knew I had seen Hugh in the grip of some sort of crisis on that stage, and brief as it might have been, by its consequences it had become serious.

During his hour of rest before leaving the theater that afternoon, Hugh told me—no, informed me—that I was to take "a little vacation."

"Indeed," I said.

He said he'd been thinking that I'd been undergoing "too much stress" (another blasted Americanism) and that I was to "go off somewhere for a month or so and"—here he paused for dramatic effect, waving the hand bearing his cigarette holder like an arrogant monarch—"regenerate."

I said I would not go, that I did not feel the need; and thought, *He's wanting to get rid of me so he can sink into some damnable abyss, and I won't leave him.*

We had a tremendous row. We called each other every conceivable name and nearly came to blows. At last Hugh wrapped himself in his flapping raincoat and said, disgustedly, "See you around, Leon," and as he slammed the door he muttered what sounded like, "That little bitch!"

While the epithet smacked of the wrong gender, I assumed he meant me, and I had no heart to follow him. He came home sixteen hours later, alone, smelling of vomit and still halfway drunk, and fell like a cracked-up toy soldier into my arms. He stayed in bed for two days, behaving like a huge, cranky infant. No further mention of my "vacation" was ever made by either of us.

So although the dream he told me that night did not seem of great moment to me, I began gingerly to piece things together. The dream had upset him, leading to his awkward performance, which had upset him further. The mysterious woman in the dream had made him feel lonely. His little mistake on stage had made him feel his age and fear a loss of power, a decline, and that had angered him. He had then tested this uncertain power on me by dictating my vacation, and when I bested him by refusing, he had become further enraged. It all made sense in a Hugh-ish sort of way, and I congratulated myself on my amateur analysis.

All this analyzing went on that night as I dozed on and

off on the chaise by Hugh's bedside. After relating his dream, he had fallen into a fitful sleep and I had dimmed the lights and removed his hands from behind his head and tucked him up like a baby. I don't know why, but I felt I should sleep there instead of going back to my room. I looked at Hugh for a minute as he lay there. In repose, his face looked almost his true age; with his blazing eyes closed he looked dignified, peaceful, and shy, and I prayed he would wake feeling better. I decided against lying down next to him (though the bed was capacious) and took to the lounge.

I thought he was off for the night, but after an hour or so he woke up and began speaking as if there had been no intermission.

"That afternoon on stage, Leon," he said after arranging his arms behind his head again and adjusting the covers. "You were quite right. . . I mean about something being wrong." This statement woke me up completely; Hugh never admitted such things. "It was that dream-woman, Leon," he continued. "She was there."

"What do you mean, 'there'?" I asked.

Amazingly, while still on his back and seeming not to move a muscle, he lit a cigarette. I brought him an ashtray and a glass of seltzer. His voice sounded cracked and dry.

"I mean she was there in the audience, Leon, *there in the bloody first row*, and Leon, SHE DID . . . IT . . . AGAIN!"

At this he popped straight up out of bed, spilling the drink, upsetting the ashtray, and giving me quite a start. He dragged the bedspread with him, pulling it around him like a cape, and began to stalk about the room as if he were searching for something. He waved his cigarette holder in his impatient, imperial way.

"Sit down, Hugh," I begged him. "What are you looking for?"

He plopped down nearly on top of me on the chaise and handed me the cigarette. He put his arm around me, he put his head on my shoulder. I didn't look down and I didn't hear a thing, but I wondered if Hugh had begun to cry.

10. Nora

Life after the play was like a new life. I spent the first few days after my return from New York in a kind of dizzy reverie; I could think of nothing but that magical afternoon. Even after that first flush faded, Hugh still stood on the edge of my mind like a patron saint or guardian angel who could hop into the action whenever called upon or needed. On the surface, I suppose I seemed normal, but I felt as if I had changed. It was like being in love, only without that hopeless, terrified feeling that the loved one might not return your affections, because in this case of course there was no chance of that, and actually no real desire for it either. I thought of Hugh not as a person I might possibly come to know but as an experience that had altered my larger view. If anything, I bet I appeared more cheerful; at one point, in fact, Rick commented on how "carefree" I was acting, and I told him the weekend had done me good, that I'd needed to get away.

I felt like drawing all the time, but whenever I tried,

things got messed up; I didn't really have a theme to work on. Then, one evening, everything came together. Rick wasn't home, our apartment building was quiet, and I took a sketchpad out onto the back porch. It was almost too dark to see, but I worked very quickly for about two hours before I really even knew what I was doing. When I decided to take a break and went in to make some tea, taking the drawing with me, I was amazed at what I saw under the bright kitchen lights.

Here was the drawing I had imagined—the drawing of the inside of the theater that afternoon—and it was just the way I'd seen it in my mind's eye. I remembered thinking, driving home from New York that day, that the picture would be like an illustration for a Wilkie Collins novel, old-fashioned and haunting, composed of a network of fine lines. The picture I held in my hand was certainly my work, but I had hardly been conscious of its execution; it was as if all my thoughts of the past few days had somehow given their energy and rapture to the original idea I'd had that day in the car.

As I drank my tea I noted a few changes and additions I wanted to make. There should be just a bit of color: the palest of golds for the area extending from Hugh to me (I was just the back of a head in the first row), and exactly the right kind of "black" for Hugh's eyes. What pleased me most was the excitement generated by the vibration of so many precisely drawn, delicate lines, and the way the lighted area of the stage and the beam of "golden air" allowed the observer to see into the front of the audience just enough for a mystery to develop there. I went back outside and finished the drawing quickly (I had some trouble with the eyes, but finally hit upon putting in pinpoints of white and blue, which illuminated their blackness perfectly), brought it into my room, matted it, and set it face down on top of the bookcase. I didn't want to look at it anymore that night.

I was suddenly very tired, but as I started preparing for

bed I had a brilliant idea: I would send the drawing to Hugh Sheenan with a short thank-you letter. It was the perfect gift. I did not hope for a reply (in fact I really didn't even want one), but I thought perhaps it was an offering unusual enough to get past his secretary and into his own hands. I loved the idea that he might look at it with pleasure, or even that he might touch it before setting it forever aside or giving it to someone to dispose of. (If I thought that Hugh might actually see the picture, I wouldn't even care that it might be destroyed.)

That night as I drifted happily off to sleep, I composed a letter to Hugh in my mind. I would keep it simple. For once, I wouldn't worry about the awkwardness of my prose. The drawing would speak for me.

Dear Mr. Sheenan:

I will be brief, since I imagine you receive oceans of mail. I was fortunate enough to be present at the matinee performance of The Lion's Share *one Sunday afternoon a few weeks ago, and I had to write to thank you. I have followed your career for many years, and as soon as I heard about the play I made plans to drive down from Boston to see you. I cannot tell you how wonderful that afternoon was for me; you, and all the members of the cast, were marvelous, and filled my heart with joy.*

I wanted to give you something in return, but could think of nothing appropriate until one day I completed the enclosed drawing. Acting is what you do superbly; drawing is what I do best, so in some small way I hope you will accept my offering as a fair exchange. Perhaps it will bring you at least a moment of pleasure.

With all best wishes for your continued health and success, and with deepest gratitude, I remain,

Yours truly,

Nora Forrest

I wrote it on our old typewriter. I typed a clean copy. I agonized a little, but then I packed up the drawing with the letter and addressed it all to the theater, the only place I could think of that made any sense. I mailed it the next morning. I knew I'd be wondering about it a lot, and thinking about it was tantalizingly scary, but I felt good. I'd done what I could and that was that. The letter would not be, should not be, answered. In my imagination, Hugh's secretary passed the package on to him; he read the letter and smiled, he looked at the drawing, and looked and looked again. He had it framed and hung on the wall of his London study as a curiosity that interested him for a reason he didn't understand. Sometimes he would look at it and remember his days in New York and wonder who in the world the "N.F." whose initials were in the corner of the drawing might be.

I am not a fool; I knew none of that was at all likely to happen. But I loved to pretend that it might.

11. Leon

Hugh was ordinarily a late riser, and over the years I'd come to bless that habit. The early mornings were mine alone, and I especially loved them in New York, where the days began not exactly with perfect peace and quiet but at least with a minimum of noise and a lovely view of rooftops and wires and the Hudson River off in the distance, sparkling as if it knew no human blight. I'd brew a pot of the tea I'd brought from home and read the papers end to end, scanning always for a mention of Hugh and, I admit, censoring a number of clippings from his view.I had boxes and boxes of his clippings and I saved everything, but I didn't like to upset him unnecessarily, more for my own protection than his. The slightest criticism of the play disturbed him in those days (unusual for him), and there were a couple or three of theater gossip-columnists whose inventions or exaggerations of what they'd seen or heard seemed to Hugh invasions of privacy so egregious that they must be dealt with swiftly and by the sword. Once he had rung up a silly woman reporter from a restaurant where he'd picked up a paper, asked her address (which she'd willingly given—expecting, no doubt, some romantic interest, or at the very least an exclusive interview), and told her he was coming right over in a cab to "cram a copy of the rag" containing her slanderous remarks "right down [her] wrinkled bloody throat." I feared for what the next day's "rag" would contain, but oddly enough, there was no mention of the episode.

Also in the mornings I'd open Hugh's mail—or, to be more precise, I'd open whatever seemed not too personal. Ruby's little letters, unmistakably addressed in her child's hand, would be placed immediately onto his breakfast tray; other letters from England would be sorted according to sender, and some of these would go onto the tray as well. I opened all business letters and fan mail. Sometimes I recalled the days when his biggest film, a war saga, had brought sacks and sacks of mail from the studio, letters from all over the world, in many different languages. Eventually we'd been forced to hire a gaggle of secretaries to answer them and mail out "autographed" pictures of Hugh in his film character's military uniform. (Hugh always hated the sight of those letters; he hadn't liked the film that much himself. Once he set fire to three bundles of them in the garden's empty birdbath before I could stop him.) In more recent years there had been usually only five or six letters a month, though since the beginning of this Broadway engagement there had been more, especially at first. Somehow New Yorkers always found out where one was, and many letters came directly to us at the hotel.

I handled these letters myself, rarely calling any to Hugh's attention. People sent things, too: blue gloves, for the most part, and occasionally baked goods, books, or photographs for Hugh to sign. I signed these with his name, since he would not do it. Now and then he'd ask, "Is my public still writing me, Leon?" and seemed satisfied with a yes, though I suspected a no would not have upset him unduly.

I will not say I was jaded, but I'd been at this game so long that it took a great deal to surprise or even interest me. In the early years, when letters were especially generous or amusing, or when the writer seemed in dire need of Hugh's personal touch (sick people, especially children, would always succeed in getting his attention, for example), I'd leave them on the desk for Hugh to peruse. Occasionally he would have me send theater tickets to someone, or write something nice on a photograph and ask me to send it "posthaste" (I think he thought that was some kind of Postal Service designation). But of late years Hugh had not been at all interested, so I had taken over the task completely, using my discretion as to which fans would receive a more personal reply, always penned by me. I'd felt awful about that at first, but had come to reason that it would make people happy and they'd never know the truth at any rate.

This particular morning the post held nothing more than rubbish mail, some credit card bills, and a medium-large flat package done up in brown paper. It had been addressed to the theater and forwarded to the hotel. The thing was uncommonly stiff, and the return address was simply "Forrest" at a location in Boston. Hugh and I had visited Boston once years before, but it had been a very quick trip and to my knowledge he had no real friends there. And, I reasoned, trying to decide whether to open the package or not, no real friend would write to him at the theater. So I opened it.

A letter on cheap stationery fell out, but I did not bother to read it. There was a drawing inside, matted on stiff cardboard and wound in a sheet of tissue, and I undid the wrapping and propped the drawing up against the teapot for examination.

I am no connoisseur of art—that's Hugh's department. His house in London is filled with paintings, sculptures, glass, and pottery from all over the world, each costly piece selected lovingly by himself or his first wife. None of it offends me, but it brings me no real joy to speak of. There was something about this drawing, however, that hooked me in.

I supposed at first that it was another purchase of Hugh's, but then realized that such a purchase would never have been posted in such a flimsy wrapper, or sent to the theater address at that. I sipped my tea and I sipped that drawing. It was the strangest-looking thing. I thought it might be an antique, considering its style, but the paper on which it was rendered was very new indeed, and the color, where there was color, was too vivid, and the whites too white, to be old.

It was a picture of the inside of a theater, seen from a vantage point somewhere in the upper rear, with a stage full of actors, well-lit in the front, and a tall, thin male actor at the front of the stage with a peculiar look on his face. A shaft or beam of light, like something one sees in those Roman Catholic holy cards that nuns give out to children for good behavior in school,led from the actor's dark eyes (which gleamed with an unearthly, almost electric, light) to something in the front rows of the audience. The detail was most unusual: the whole of the thing was executed in an elegant array of tiny, finely drawn lines, so that unless one looked closely it seemed to have a palpable texture; one felt as though it would be a bit rough to the touch. Most of the drawing was simply black on white, but the beam of light was a soft golden color and, as I mentioned, the man's eyes, though black, seemed to have a color all their own. Down in the lower right-hand corner of the picture were the initials "N.F."

So deeply was I in communion with this strange drawing that Hugh's unexpected entry into the kitchen gave me rather a start. He was wearing an old, fuzzy, grey bathrobe, had an unattractive greyish-blue stubble on his chin, and his eyes were sunken deeply enough into his face so that he looked about a hundred and three years old. He seemed cheerful enough in spite of that, however, and considering that the hour was well before noon, I thought he seemed very cheerful indeed. He smiled at me and croaked one word—"Coffee"—then plopped down at the table next to me, leaned over almost backwards, and acrobatically lit his cigarette in its holder by turning on the stove. I did not argue about the coffee, for once, I was that surprised to see him; I simply got up to fix him a mug.

"And what have we here, old boy?" he asked, picking up the drawing and trying to focus his bleary eyes upon it. "Dabbling in the arts, are we, Leon? I have always wondered what it was one did in these early hours, but I must say you'd be the last silly bastard I'd suspect of finger painting. HOLD ON!" At that Hugh jumped from the chair, threw the drawing across the room as if it had burned him, and turned upon me with a hateful eye. He was indeed fully awakened.

"For God's sake, Leon! Where did that thing come from?" he roared.

I was flabbergasted. "It came just this morning in the post. I was just taking a little look-see at it when you came in."

Hugh retrieved the drawing from where it had landed, set it up again against the teapot, sat down, and gazed at it with his head in his hands. His cigarette, abandoned, had fallen to his lap and was starting a hole there. I took it away to the sink. He continued to stare at the picture, muttering foul words and bending a spoon in his hands. I took the spoon away.

"Wouldn't you like to tell me what's going on?" I asked.

He looked at me as if I were daft. Then he smiled, radiantly. "Coffee," he commanded.I served him his mug.

"Leon," he said in a syrupy, mocking tone, "can you really not identify what you see here just before you?" He gestured at the painting, noticed his cigarette was missing from its holder, and lit another, this time from a lighter produced from his robe's pocket.

"Indeed not," I said. "I was looking at the thing because it was so very odd. . . not because I was trying to 'identify' it. What is it, anyway?"

Again I received the cold and mocking stare. "Where is the package this came in?" Hugh asked.

I gave him the torn brown paper.

"And was there nothing else?" he inquired. He downed the mug of coffee in one gulp and banged it on the table, signaling for more. Not being an idiot, I gave him an instant refill.

It was only then I remembered the letter that had fallen out of the wrapping. During all the ruckus it had been knocked to the floor, and I picked it up and handed it to Hugh.

His face changed from sneering to terrorized. "Have you read it?"

I told him no.

He handed it back to me. "Then read it to me now," he said, and he couldn't have looked more resigned to a beastly blow than had I held a telegram bringing certain news of death or disaster.

The letter I read to him was nothing special at all: some woman (probably young, I thought) had written to thank him for his performance in *The Lion's Share*, which she had seen some weeks before, and had enclosed a drawing of her own as a little gift. It was a simple, polite letter—short and, I thought, rather nice on the whole, especially for an American. It was signed "Nora Forrest" and the return address in Boston was given again, as is only proper. The writer asked for nothing, and I certainly approved of that.

Hugh said not a word when I finished reading, but simply reached out for the letter, folded it twice over, and put it immediately into his pocket. He kept a hand on that pocket while he finished his coffee, as if he were afraid the letter would escape. He continued to contemplate the drawing. I knew better than to speak.

After a while he rose, put his mug in the sink, ran water in it (I had never seen him do anything so domestic before), and asked me quite quietly how long it would take to "have something framed."

I said I supposed it could be done in a day or two.

"Bugger," he said. "Then measure this thing for me, will you Leon, and go buy a ready-made frame right away. After you've measured it, bring it upstairs. I'll be in the bath." Then he exited the room, with great drama, as if on stage. The second cigarette had burned a tidy little dimple in the hotel's table.

I purchased a frame for the drawing and put it all together. Much to my amazement, Hugh insisted on carrying the thing around with him everywhere for several days. He took it from room to room, always propping it up in some prominent place but rarely, it seemed, actually looking at it. At the theater it reposed on his dressing table, and when it came near time for him to go on stage, he'd tuck it in the closet. He'd take it out again when the play was over, then slip it into a large plastic bag and carry it with him to the car. I was never allowed to touch it, and the few times I asked him about it I received no reply. His mood was consistently distracted, though not disagreeable, and I was content to humor this minor obsession of his, knowing that sooner or later the story would out.

After about a week, there was a development.

"Leon," Hugh said to me one evening as I brushed some hairs from his jacket, "this drawing has been disturbing me a very great deal."

"I know," I said. "Would you like to tell me about it?"

He ignored the question, which did not surprise me, and asked, "Do you think this Miss Nora Whoever might have a telephone?"

"I expect so, Hugh," I answered. "Most people do."

"Then please find the number."

That was easy enough. When I brought it to him on a slip of paper he simply looked at it and said, "I see." Into the pocket went the paper.

The next evening, after his bath, he asked me, "Leon, would you do me a favor, old man, and see if this number will ring?" He handed me the piece of paper.

"I'm sure it will ring, Hugh. Would you like me to try it for you?"

"Yes."

"Now?"

"Please."

So I picked up the phone by his bed, dialed the number, heard the first ring, then handed him the phone. He listened momentarily, then put the receiver back on its stand.

"Thank you, Leon." And then he went to bed.

This idiocy continued for another day or so. Each night we would ring up the woman in Boston, and each time Hugh would hang up the phone. Then one evening I refused to make the call.

"Why are you disturbing this person?" I asked him. "Don't you think it rather rude to ring someone's number every night and then hang up? Perhaps the poor woman thinks someone dreadful is after her. I don't understand all this, Hugh; it seems to me very silly."

He handed me the little scrap of paper. "Call it again," he said.

I said no, thank you very much, I was finished with this foolish business; I was going to bed.

"Dial it, Leon," he told me. "Dial it and if she answers, tell her I received her letter and the drawing. Tell her I'm going to be in Boston next Monday"—there were no performances on Mondays—"and that I would like to meet her for lunch." He paused, breathing heavily. "She will probably accept. Make whatever arrangements necessary for the trip, Leon, and kindly do not look at me as if I were some bloody loon." He turned off the lamp next to his bed and crawled into it. "Call from the other room," he said, "and let me know what happened in the morning."

I was outraged, fascinated, puzzled, and amused. I made the call. The woman answered on the third ring. I told her Mr. Hugh Sheenan had received her package and requested the honor of her presence at the Ritz-Carlton for luncheon the following Monday at one o'clock, and asked whether I could send a car for her. There was a long silence. Then, thank you, she said, but she would meet Mr. Sheenan at the Ritz; she did not require a car. She sounded not at all surprised, but rather vague—completely emotionless and polite. I said, how would we know her? She said she'd be wearing a yellow dress and that she had "sort of long" light hair. She thanked me twice for calling.

In the morning, when I passed Hugh's open door on my way to the kitchen, he was sitting up in bed, smoking. I reported the conversation.

"Thank you, Leon," he said, and then, "A yellow dress." For the rest of the day he was quiet but nervy, and I do not think he slept that week at all.

12. Nora

Writing to Hugh Sheenan, and sending the drawing, had been a kind of exorcism. I'd worried that I'd do nothing but wonder what had happened to my package, but instead I felt a huge sense of relief—as if I'd accomplished something extremely difficult and frightening. Although I went on thinking about the play, it was no longer with the same sense of urgency. I felt, in a way, that it was mine at last; I had lost a great part of the anxiety that my memories would escape.

And so life settled down to a pleasing normal. Rick and I were getting along well, we were healthy, our jobs were satisfactory, we had no real worries. In bed, my mind and body had fully returned to Rick. That statement might be misleading; the truth is that at no time, before seeing *The Lion's Share* or after, had I ever fantasized about Hugh as an actual lover. But it was also true that in those first weeks following the play, I was but a distant partner for Rick. I think he must have noticed, but when you've been with someone a very long time you get used to variations in passion—it's something that waxes and wanes. My feelings for Rick never changed, and I did not compare him to Hugh, but I was a mass of distractions. I dreamed of Hugh a good deal in those days, and though the one dream I desperately wanted to experience again, the dream of him falling from the roof, never returned, I would go to bed at night hoping for at least a glimpse of him, or even a conversation with him, in some dream meeting. The power of auto-suggestion being strong in me, I was able on many occasions to actually hold these tête-à-têtes with a Hugh who had become familiar and dear to me, a Hugh largely of my own creation. My imaginary friend. I was fully conscious of this element of fantasy, and it seemed no more harmful to me than novel reading or other forms of escape.

No one knew the extent of my dabbling in this little hobby, which made it all the more precious. Realizing that my intense enthusiasm would make me look a little foolish, upon my return from New York I had told people how much I'd enjoyed the play, and seeing Hugh in person, but had toned down my elation to a more-or-less dignified degree. If the occasional day did go by when I was too busy to have a moment's reflection on Hugh, I'd later think, *I've been away from you too long*, and greet my next thought or dream of him with the joyous salute of one coming home after an enforced absence. Was it obsession? I think of the word as a pejorative term—for a mysterious fascination, in this case—but I suppose there are people who would call it that. There's another psychological term, the "ghostly lover" syndrome, or fixation on an imaginary relationship with an ideal romantic counterpart, but that didn't fit perfectly either. I knew enough about Hugh to know he was far from the ideal partner, and to realize that even were circumstances outlandish enough to bring us together, we would never have "gotten along." My connection with him was an affinity based on something outside psychology, and while I didn't place it distinctly in the realm of the psychic, I suppose it was closer to that than to anything else—or anything we have a label for. Call it "spiritual," perhaps. Ever since I'd first seen him, he'd been undeniably there—not chosen or elected from any gallery of possible soulmates, but simply. . . recognized.

After I mailed the drawing, I thought the circle was complete. In a way I wished that I'd taken a photograph of it so it would not be so irrevocably gone from my life, but in another way its absence made the sacrifice sweeter. I would never try to draw the same picture again.

13. Rick

Of course I knew she still loved me, but my Nora had gone away. She wasn't always there for me behind those funny eyes, and although she did all the things she always did, and was as cheerful as I could want her to be, she moved in a kind of private world that began to shut me out more and more.

I'm speaking about the weeks after she went to see that play. It was the only event I could pin these changes on, and it seemed, in ways I found hard to define, the only possible explanation. I knew, too, that the missing drawing was in some way involved, but strange as it may now seem, it did not occur to me for quite a while that the drawing was connected to the play.

When it finally hit me I felt like the stupidest of fools. The tall man, of course, was her idol, Hugh Sheenan. But what was it all about—that shaft of light, for instance? I had no idea.

Once, when Nora wasn't home, and her mother called to chat, I asked her casually about the play. She was eager to describe what a fine time they'd had, what a lovely dinner afterwards, and what good seats they'd been lucky enough to obtain. I then remembered Nora saying (she'd probably told me a hundred times in fact) that they'd been sitting in the front row, and how magical it had all seemed to her, being up so close.

So I decided that Nora had drawn the picture of Hugh Sheenan looking down into the first row of the audience. . . at her. This put me a little at ease, and took some of the sinister mystery out of the picture; it made it seem a harmless fantasy, an innocent schoolgirl daydream. And sometimes, when Nora's spaciness was really starting to annoy me and I was thinking about criticizing her for something, I'd remember how dear she was to me, and how imperfect I was, and how she rarely complained about my smoking, my lateness, my sloppiness around the house. And I'd think of that drawing, and I wouldn't say a thing. I wished I could see it again, and then again I didn't. I was comfortable with my analysis of the drawing and of Nora's state of mind, and I think I knew that if I saw that picture again it would so disturb me that I wouldn't feel so comfortable anymore.

Anyway, after a couple of weeks, Nora started changing back into her old self. The only remnant of her preoccupied air was that she was slightly absent-minded about things, which was most unusual for her. Once she lost her keys, the ones she kept on a silver ring with a little crystal dangling from it, and when, the next day, I found them in a kitchen drawer, I teased her about hiding them there unconsciously, and began to call her Magpie. She was happy with that—she seemed even happy that she'd misplaced the keys, that she'd been capable of such forgetfulness—and we made love that afternoon twice, a thing we hadn't done for years and years.

14. Hugh

I used to read a lot more than I do now. I used to remember a lot more too. But one quote I do remember, or misremember, possibly from Guy de Maupassant, is this: "Often the truth is sometimes not probable." It's the kind of quote one likes without really knowing why, until one day its significance bashes one smack in the solar plexus. When Leon showed me the drawing that arrived in the post that day, I knew in my heart of hearts what that funny quote meant.

It was that fucking, bloody, brazen woman from the play, of course. I knew it before Leon read me her quaint little letter. A picture is worth a thousand words indeed. Poor Leon. He didn't know what the hell was going on; probably never did really find out. But how could I tell him? What would I say? "Oh Leon, dear boy, it's the woman from the dream. You know, old chap, the woman from the first row, the one who almost made me fall on my arse in the third act. Lovely drawing, don't you think? Let's have another look at it over dessert."

He might have tried to make me see a shrink (he did try, now and then, but so far had not succeeded; I protected my anomalies from all outside interference—I was quite fond of them). True, I had told Leon about the dream, and about what had happened to me that night onstage, but I think (luckily for me) he had taken it all as the ravings of a man with too little sleep and too much imagination. He is far too practical a bloke to believe that I believed what I had told him.

When I began to trundle that picture around with me in its terrible frame (all Leon's taste, as they say, is in his mouth; one can pass as a successful autodidact and still never develop any aesthetic sensibility to speak of), I suppose he thought it was just another eccentricity of mine; I sincerely doubt that he made any connection with the dream or the theatre incident, and I was just as happy to keep it that way. I know he disapproved of my making a luncheon date with a stranger, but in long-ago years I had done such a thing once or twice, so it was not an act entirely without precedent.

But of course, it really was that, to me. I was already frightened of this woman, and horribly angry with her. I envisioned myself at lunch, smiling seductively at Miss Nora F., waiting until she'd become comfortable with me, then upending an entire steaming luncheon onto her small and dreadful yellow bosom. All I wanted was to ask her why she wouldn't leave me alone, but I lacked the courage to do so on the phone. I thought if I saw her in person I'd have my balls about me, and that I'd be able to reduce her, in a matter of minutes, to a quivering wreck. I wanted to hurt her. I knew I could tear her apart with my tongue. I could do that to anyone; it was the one talent I'd never had to work on. She'd begin to cry over my insults at some early point during the meal, I imagined, and I would be free to, disgustedly, leave.

The trouble was, I still believed she must be a witch.

How had she gotten from the dream to the audience, how had she beguiled me to look at her from the stage, and how had she managed to render the scene so (I had to admit it) beautifully on paper? I felt so mixed up, so utterly fouled by my puzzlement, that I had trouble with the play all week—oh, not so anyone would notice, but enough to give me one headache after another. Also, I could not sleep, and I remembered to worry about my heart.

I looked forward to the Monday the way one looks forward to a tooth extraction: it would be highly unpleasant, but later, I hoped, the pain would be gone.

15. Nora

It was awfully late at night for the phone to ring. I was in the kitchen, straightening up. Rick had stayed late at the office, then gone out with one of his friends. I considered not answering it, then decided it must be either a wrong number or something very important. It was the latter.

"Miss Forrest?" said a low-pitched voice with a British accent. Not exactly an upper-class accent, but pleasing.

"Yes," I said, intrigued.

"Excuse me, please, for bothering you at this hour. My name is Graves, and I am Mr. Hugh Sheenan's personal secretary. I have a message for you from Mr. Sheenan."

My heart and lungs flew out from my chest and splattered all over my shoes. The floor was thick with gore. I had nothing to breathe with, so I did not say a word.

"Mr. Sheenan," the voice continued, sounding very formal, "having received your letter and gift, requests the honor of your presence at luncheon at the Boston Ritz-Carlton this coming Monday at one o'clock. May I send a car 'round to fetch you?"

I could not think or speak; I believe I came close to fainting. I remember looking at the lamp on the kitchen table, seeing some dust around its base, and saying to myself, *You'll have to clean that.* I had a death grip on the phone, and only when the cramp in my hand woke me from my stupor was I able to answer Mr. Graves.

"Thank you," I said, in a small voice, but calmly. "I will meet Mr. Sheenan at the hotel dining room. I won't need a car."

"As you wish, Miss Forrest. And may I ask how we shall know you, since you and Mr. Sheenan have not met?"

"Not met" indeed, I thought. *Mr. Sheenan will know me*. But to the man on the phone I said, "Oh. I'll be wearing a yellow dress. And my hair is light and sort of long." I sounded all of fifteen.

"Thank you, Miss Forrest. Until Monday, then." And he hung up.

I hung up too, then went to the sink, moistened a paper towel, cleaned the base of the lamp, and put on some water to boil.

I sat down. Then I got up and made tea. *This is awful*, was my first conscious thought. This is awful, I have to work Monday. How did this happen? This was not supposed to happen. I knew I shouldn't have put a return address on the envelope, but it seemed so tacky not to, and anyway I never, never, never expected a response. Especially a response like this—a form letter maybe, an autographed photo maybe—but never anything ever like this. This was awful. And I had accepted, accepted without batting an eye. *I must be crazy*, I thought. *My head must really hold a whole cartload of loose screws*.

I had to get to bed before Rick came home and found me sitting there looking goofy; I had no desire to answer any questions. So I took myself off to try and sleep, though of course it was hopeless. When Rick came in I feigned unconsciousness, and he kissed me lightly on the head and fell asleep instantly himself. I cuddled into him, and took his hand and held it to my heart for a while, but I could not still my mind. No useful thoughts were forming there, but all sorts of things were circling madly, making my closed eyes ache. My one ray of hope was that the call had been a hoax—but how could it have been? Maybe Rick had found someone with an accent and convinced him to call. But Rick would never try to make a fool of me, I knew that, and anyway it wasn't the kind of "joke" that would ever cross his mind. It wasn't funny enough, for one thing. And who else would do it?

I knew the caller had been real. His name was Graves, and he had given me a message from Hugh Sheenan, who wanted me to have "luncheon" with him at the Ritz. Oh God, it was awful, and I had said yes. I wished I would just wake up and realize the whole thing had been a nightmare designed to teach me a lesson. You know how people say, "Be careful what you ask for"? Had I begged for this without realizing what I was doing? It was all my fault. I still had a few days of reprieve. Maybe I would die before I had to face him.

But I did not die. And I did not tell anyone about the phone call. I came very close to telling my best friend, Mellie, and I thought very seriously about telling Rick, but in the end I just couldn't. Even if they believed me, they would want to know exactly how the man had come to call. And I couldn't tell anyone about the letter and the drawing; it was too personal. Also, I was too embarrassed.

Instead of wanting to tell the world that I was going to have lunch with a famous movie star, I wanted to bury the fact as deeply as possible underground. I considered not going, but I couldn't do that either; I felt as if I were caught up in some kind of scripted plot that absolutely had to be followed.

So I arranged to take the day off from work, and to cover all bases I told Rick I was taking a vacation day to go up to Gloucester and visit Mellie. I told Mellie that if Rick called (which I doubted he would), she should say I had taken her children to the beach, and that she was just fixing some food to bring there too.

Mellie was surprised, but agreed to do it. "Nora," she said. "You're not having an affair?"

I think I convinced her that was ridiculous, though I couldn't blame her for asking. I did not feel guilty about all this deception; I felt I was protecting Rick from knowing what an incredible dimwit he had married.

And then I began to worry about how I would look, what I would say, and other such potentially planet-changing things. I realized I'd have to wear the yellow dress, because I'd told Mr. Graves that I would, and anyway it was my best outfit. I was, hour by hour, growing more apprehensive. I still did not understand why this singular invitation had come my way, but it was clear that I would have to honor my acceptance of it. There was no way out. I clung to the hope that there would be a number of other fans there and that I could get lost among them—maybe Hugh Sheenan was in the habit of flying to Boston once a week just to entertain his admirers? Fat chance; what I knew about him made that idea absurd.

I was so scared I felt nauseous almost all the time, and I wondered how, even if I managed to get to the hotel, I would ever be able to eat anything. How could I possibly even *speak* to Hugh Sheenan? He was older, he was a creative genius, he wasn't even American, and, worst of all by far, he must already think I'm a terrible fool. I remembered the anger and confusion in his eyes that afternoon in the theater and I wondered if there would be some kind of dues to pay for that. But maybe, just maybe, he hadn't connected that afternoon in the theater with the drawing; maybe it was all in my mind, and this was just some freak occurrence; perhaps he had simply liked the drawing and was just a kind soul who happened to have a spare luncheon hour to spend with a struggling artist. I didn't believe that, but I tried to. Oh why had I done it, done any of it?

But there was nothing to do but to go. The week passed somehow. On Monday morning, after Rick left for work, I took a long shower, fixed myself up as best I could, put on the yellow dress, and sat down, wretched, for three hours. I smoked so many of Rick's cigarettes, and made my throat so sore, I doubted I would be able to speak to Hugh Sheenan even if I could think of anything to say. I drank about four cups of strong tea as well; I coughed and ran to the bathroom repeatedly. I envisioned the coming unraveling of my life's most humiliating moments.

The whole thing was impossible, and I was completely on my own. I had neglected even to ask Mr. Graves where to go when I got to the Ritz. How was I supposed to find the right dining room? (Never having been inside the place, I pictured it as labyrinthine, mysterious.) And then, how was I to announce myself? I should have taken him up on his offer of the car, which would have at least provided me with some sort of protection from complete awkwardness, but then I would have had to explain its presence to any of my neighbors who might have seen it.

What worried me most, I suppose, even more than the fear that I was in for a terrible tongue-lashing by one of the world's most excoriating wits, was that I would be struck dumb as a piece of shingle and come off as a pitiful dolt in his dark and brilliant eyes. It never, in my selfish agonies, occurred to me to think of what Hugh Sheenan might be feeling; I felt my significance too small to merit much importance in his thoughts. His reasons for inviting me to lunch were puzzling, but he was entitled to any eccentricity, as far as I was concerned. It was all my fault, not Hugh's.

Then it was time to leave. I checked the mirror about five hundred times, but all I could see there was that strange, pale-mouthed, ageless woman again, the one I'd first seen in the bathroom of the bar across from the theater. Whoever she was, she was in serious trouble now.

16. Leon

Hugh had pulled some odd ones in his time, but this luncheon in Boston was one of the oddest in my memory. I didn't understand a thing about it. Oh, I knew it had something to do with the drawing and the theater and the dream Hugh had described to me, but I couldn't fit it all together—he was keeping the key to the puzzle just out of my reach. But as I observed him in those days between the extension of his invitation to Miss Forrest and the luncheon itself, I realized that he was not ignoring me on purpose; he had simply become so wound up in all the mysterious goings-on that he had forgotten about me altogether.

He did ask me, several times, if I'd made reservations for the trip to Boston, and each time I assured him I had. Feeling in my bones that Hugh was going to need even more privacy than usual on this little jaunt, I had booked six seats on the airline shuttle (ours plus two empty ones in back of and in front of us); arranged for the most private of suites at the Ritz; informed the hotel management that Mr. Sheenan would only be in town for a very few hours, on a matter that required the utmost privacy, and cautioned them against leaking our arrival to the press (fortunately, hotel people seem to keep their lips fairly well-buttoned when the stakes are high); hired a reputable but unostentatious car and driver in Boston; and refilled all the prescriptions in my little black bag. When I went to close Hugh's valise that morning I found he had slipped in two full bottles of bourbon, which I emptied down the drain.

He had ceased, at last, to carry the drawing around with him—outside the hotel, that is. While at home, he would still transport it from room to room, almost absent-mindedly, as if out of lifelong habit. He was not sleeping well, and when he finally did struggle out of bed in the mornings he would slip on a pair of old reading glasses and go over to the bureau and examine the drawing, as if he suspected it had changed somehow in the night. Sometimes he'd touch it with one finger, tracing the gold-lit area and then looking at his hand as if he suspected the color would come off and stain him.

The night before our trip to Boston he did not even attempt to go to bed until almost two in the morning. Ordinarily, I would have slipped off much earlier myself, but I thought I might as well stay up that night and see if I could learn anything. I had the feeling there was a lot I ought to know in order to be able to help Hugh through what promised to be, in one way or another, an exhausting tomorrow.

He was sitting up in bed in his fuzzy old robe, chain-smoking, drinking quantities of cherry soda, and leafing aimlessly through magazines. Finally, I said to him, "Hugh, you've got to try to sleep. Our plane leaves La Guardia at seven, though God knows why we have to leave so early."

"Go to bed, Leon. I'll be fine."

"Let me change the reservation to ten; surely that will leave us plenty of time."

He looked at me coolly. "I wish to depart on the seven o'clock, thank you. I would not care to be late for lunch—one never knows what kind of delays one will meet while traveling."

When Hugh said "I wish to," there was no arguing.

"All right then," I told him, "I'll call you at five," and I headed for my room.

"One thing, dear Leon," Hugh called after me.

I turned.

"You may not think I know what I'm doing tomorrow, but I do. I am going to rid myself of a monkey on my back. The monkey is this Forrest woman. You must leave me to do that work alone."

"Meaning?"

"Meaning that I do not wish you to join us for lunch, if you don't mind." He gave me what was no doubt supposed to be a fearsome stare.

I did my best to look as though I concurred. "As you wish." I had no intention of leaving him alone with a possible nutcase, but I would not let him know it.

"Thank you, Leon. You and I will have a fine lobster dinner tomorrow evening in Boston."

I nodded and took myself off to my room, thinking how I would convince him that he really oughtn't eat anything so rich as lobster, little knowing, of course, that that particular problem would not prove a vexing one for me the next day.

I rose at four thirty, my eyes feeling like over-boiled eggs. At five precisely, after having had a quick cup, I knocked on Hugh's door. No answer. I went in. He had pulled up the blinds and was sitting at a small table in the just-breaking sunlight, sipping a large coffee he must have ordered secretly from room service and reading *The Boston Globe*, which they must have obtained for him as well. He was fully dressed in a three-piece off-white linen suit with a pale blue shirt and white tie. His blue gloves lay on the table beside him.

Curtains of sun-shot smoke hung in the air around him like a gauzy frame, and the weak early-morning light touched his black-grey hair and heavy eyebrows and illuminated the long bones of his face so that he looked like an El Greco. Although he was still too thin by far, and deep lines of fatigue were carved about his mouth and eyes, I had not seen him looking so handsome, so fine, in a very long time. He smiled at me, his eyes lit up the room, and in spite of myself, I had a little thrill, the effect was so unearthly. I knew that Hugh, like myself, had had almost no sleep at all the previous night, but somehow he had emerged from his evening vigil looking better than any mortal had a right to. The queer, ever-present drawing was leaning near him on the window ledge.

"Leon! Many happy returns of the day!" he said, rising and pulling out a chair for me. "Have a seat, old chap; join me for a moment on this marvelous morning."

"Happy returns?" I muttered. "It's not my birthday, is it?"

"Just an expression, Leon, that's all. It means 'may the day bring you many happy returns on whatever you care to invest in it' . . . or something like that. What does it matter? Who knows? Who cares? Here, have at a section of this funny foreign newspaper the maid brought me." He handed me the sports section of *The Globe*.

"You will see, Leon," he went on, "that it is baseball season in Boston. The paper says the local team is chock-a-block full of promising rookies . . . 'promising rookies,' Leon!

Isn't that a marvelous phrase? Pity we will not be here longer; I think I should like to go out to the ball field—or what do you call it? —and take a look at these 'promising rookies,' wouldn't you?"

"You hate sports, Hugh," I reminded him. His memory could be quite selective.

Hugh roared at me in his Lear voice: "Dost thou call me fool, boy?"

I wasn't fazed. "You do hate them, though."

"Ah. But Leon, that is not precisely true. What about my short but brilliant career in polo?"

He was speaking of a post-navy obsession that had lasted only a month. I think he admired the drinking capacity of the players much more than their prowess on the field. They'd liked him too.

"You broke both ankles," I said.

He laughed that head-back laugh for which he was famous. "So I did. I am clumsy. I was not a 'promising rookie,' I suppose." He laughed again. "You're right, Leon, it's the indoor life for me. Give me a comfy chair, a cozy fire, a glass of Guinness, and a beautiful woman on my lap any day! 'Promising rookies,' indeed!"

We conversed for another five minutes or so, or I should say Hugh conversed, for I was becoming increasingly sullen in inverse proportion to his rising spirits. I deeply resented his mood. I'd barely had two winks of sleep and I knew I had a hard day ahead, made harder by the fact that I knew not what would be required of me.

But at last it was time to go. I gathered up what we needed, Hugh took his old trench coat out of the closet, and then he went to the window, removed his glasses from his pocket, placed them precariously at the end of his nose, and looked fiercely into the drawing.

"Is it coming with us?" I asked.

No, he said, he would not require the drawing, and he took it and stashed it facedown beneath the bed. "It should be quite safe there," he said, smiling. "I've noticed that in most hotels my undies can repose there quite undisturbed for days."

We left for the airport in a cab. As luck would have it, the driver was a stunningly beautiful red-haired teenage girl with a dreadfully thick Bronx accent, and Hugh chatted her up incessantly for an hour in heavy traffic, handed her a fifty-dollar tip at the airport, and kissed her fondly on both cheeks. When I looked back, she was sitting on the bonnet of her cab with a stunned, lifeless expression on her face, looking like a person gravely in need of medical attention.

17. Nora

I got off the subway at Copley, walked down Boylston, then Dartmouth, then Newbury, and continued down Newbury Street to the park. I deliberately walked past the Ritz without looking at it. Once safely in the Public Garden, I took a bench facing the hotel and tried to think how best to enter the building. I guessed I looked presentable enough for the place, because many of the people going in looked pretty ordinary. *They've got a lot of money*, I told myself, *but they're just people.*

I decided to enter on the Arlington Street side, where a grandfatherly-looking doorman stood, as opposed to the Newbury side, where a young Sylvester Stallone type stood with his arms akimbo. I wanted to be precisely five minutes late—not to be fashionable, but to increase my chances of not having to wait alone in the dining room for Hugh Sheenan. Of course, that could still happen. Weren't all famous people always late? Or maybe he wouldn't show at all, which would definitely be best. I crossed my fingers. I crossed the street. I wanted to get hit by a car, but not a single one was coming.

The grandfather-doorman smiled and opened the door for me and I stepped inside. Everything looked smaller than what I'd expected. The foyer was dark and grand, a richly appointed parlor atmosphere, complete with cozy lighting and armchairs, and several older women sat here and there paging through magazines and checking their expensive watches. I walked as slowly as I could toward the desk, and then, just when I would have had to ask about the dining room, I saw a sign indicating its location.

A lovely woman at the door, dressed as if for a cocktail party, looked at me pleasantly and asked, "Luncheon for one?"

This was the hard part. Oh no, I said, I was meeting someone, and craned my neck to look past her into the dining area. Only three tables were filled. Hugh was not at any of them.

He was unmistakably absent. I turned to the woman with all the aplomb I could muster and said, "He's not here yet." I wondered if she would have me removed for loitering; had she done so, I would have been profoundly grateful.

At that very moment I felt my left arm being very nearly wrenched from its shoulder. Hugh Sheenan had come up behind me, taken hold of my elbow with one of his enormous hands, and pulled me forward a good three feet beyond the hostess. She looked a little put out.

"Not to worry, darling," he told her. "We'll sit in the back." And he pulled me, tripping and running (he was merely strolling, his legs were so long), to a table behind some tall potted plants. He practically pushed me down in a chair, remained standing himself, waved across the room to a waiter, and called in a booming voice, "Bourbon, neat, a double," before flopping down in the chair across from me with a smirk on his face.

It was the first chance I'd really had to look at him.

The room was darkish for midday, but Hugh gave out his own light. He had on an off-white suit and vest, and a white tie against a light blue shirt that brought out all the fire in his incredible eyes. The whites of his eyes were slightly bloodshot, but the irises shone out like searchlights, ignited by some inner, invincible spark. His jacket hung loosely about him; he was ethereally thin, and so tall that even as he slumped back in his chair my eyes were only on a level with his shoulders. There was a pale blue handkerchief in his pocket that matched the shirt, and, out of keeping with all his splendor, what looked like newspaper grime all along his sleeves and cuffs. As he pulled off his pale blue gloves and laid them on the table, I thought how his long, thin fingers looked like wind chimes dangling from his wrists. His hair was a mess, and needed cutting badly, but it cast a dark shadow over his forehead that only added to the mystery of his eyes.

He was still smirking at me when the waiter came with his drink. It suddenly hit me that Hugh had recognized me—or was it only the yellow dress he'd been told to expect and the "lost" air I must have radiated in the lobby?

The waiter lit the cigarette Hugh had placed in a long black holder, and handed us some menus. "What may I bring you?" he asked me.

"She'll have a very-cherry Coke." Hugh said this in an exaggerated way, trilling the r's like a snotty butler. "A double." He laughed.

It really pissed me off. "I don't drink Coke," I said. "Vodka and tonic with lime." The waiter nodded and left.

Hugh's expression changed slightly. "Very good," he said, "I suppose you cannot be as young as you look. Or act," he added grimly.

"I'm over thirty-five," I said, idiotically. I wanted to crawl under my chair.

He grimaced. "As. Am. I."

My drink arrived.

"Look here," Hugh said. "Miss Forrest. I don't intend to beat about the bush. I invited you to lunch here today to look you over, to satisfy myself that a witch would eat real food and wouldn't speak in riddles. Let us order, so I can at least be sure of the former."

He called the waiter back and, without even glancing at me, ordered a veal dish for both of us.

I stopped him. "I don't eat meat," I said, and quickly scanned the menu for something that wouldn't make me instantly ill. I needed some protective padding in my stomach. "I'll have the pasta."

The man went away.

"You don't drink Coke and you don't eat meat," Hugh said menacingly. "What is it you *do* do? When you're not trotting around going to plays and drawing funny pictures, that is?"

He was more than beginning to get to me. I could feel tears starting to clog up my nose and make my neck as rigid as a golf club. I was determined not to cry, so I said nothing.

"Cat got your tongue?" he asked airily, waving his cigarette around like a wand.Everything he said sounded like Shakespeare. He paused so long on the final "t" of "cat" and "got" that even the cliché was unexpected.

It was too much. "I'm leaving," I said, pushing the chair back. The tears started. "I don't know why I came here. I don't know why I've liked you so long. You're stupid, you're rude, you're cruel, and you're vulgar. You asked me here to make a fool of me—I suppose I should have suspected."

I left all dignity behind. "What was my crime?" I said to him, now crying openly, enormous tears splotting all over the front of my dress. "What was my crime, that I admired you? That I wrote you a letter, that I sent you something precious to me? You're beautiful and brilliant and talented, and I found that inspiring, is that so wrong? Why didn't you leave it alone?" I sputtered. "And let me tell you something else: you don't frighten me with your Irish-macho temper—I've been around Irishmen all my life. You're not such a big deal in that department."

I was so angry my entire body hurt.

Hugh handed me a glass of water. "Sit back," he said. "I'm sorry."

"You're not," I said. "You're just surprised. You thought I would be a pitiful little twit you could have some fun with, and I'm not. I'm not fun. I'm not an idiot. And I'm going home." I got up and started to walk out of the room, amazed to see that no one was particularly looking at me. At least my outburst must have been on the quiet side, though it seemed to me as if I'd been screaming.

Hugh came after me and steered me by the elbow in another direction. "The loo is just down that aisle," he said, close to my ear; his breath felt hot as a furnace. "Don't be long."

So I washed my face and dried it on the soft, plushy hotel towels. I gave a dollar to the matron and hoped that was all right. I brushed my hair off my forehead and saw in the mirror that a little of my own face was being won back from the alien, ageless woman who had been there.I took my time, then walked carefully back to the table.

There was a small bouquet of tiny yellow roses on my plate. Fast work, I thought; the rich could manage anything. Hugh stood up. He looked like a giant boy. At his plate, a tall glass of milk stood next to the bourbon.

He held my chair and helped me to sit down. I picked up the roses and smelled them. I tried to manage a smile.

"Truly," he said, "I am sorry. I've behaved like a bastard. Since you have been honest, let me try to be honest as well." He took a swig from the milk glass, then one from the bourbon."I have been terrified of you. I have carried your drawing about with me since I received it, and I have not understood why. Let me tell you, Miss Forrest, I am not in the habit of inviting perfect strangers to lunch, and I may be quite as uncomfortable as you are, you know, though I'm sure you will not believe it." The anxious smile he gave me then was quite genuine and disarming.

"I'm sorry I called you vulgar," I said.

He laughed. "But not sorry about 'stupid,' 'rude,' and 'cruel'?"

"No," I said, also laughing, "Or 'beautiful,' 'brilliant,' or 'talented.'"

"Thank you, kind lady," he answered, bowing his head. It was like a lion's. Then he tossed it back and guffawed loudly.

"I must say, however," he said, "I don't recall ever being labeled 'Irish-macho' before."

I felt a little silly. "Well." I grinned. "It's a category I invented."

"I see," he said, eyeing me suspiciously, but still with a teasing gleam in his eye.

"Yes," I said stupidly, trying not to lose sight of reality; I realized Hugh was, deliberately or not, charming me into a state of high distraction. "But I really would like to know why you asked me here," I said. "What's all this about witches and riddles?"

"I had a dream about you," he said.

This surprised me, but apparently not enough, because Hugh was looking at me so searchingly, with such an expression of utter personal confusion on his face, that it took me aback. I tried to make light of it.

"You mean you dreamed of a person you thought I would be like," I said, like some patronizing pop-psychologist. Fear had made me lie. I'd known all along that something like this was brewing, but, like a coward witnessing a street-crime, I was determined not to become involved. Something unthinkable in the back of my mind was creeping forward on strong little legs, getting ready to clobber me with a flatiron from behind.

Our meals had arrived, and they sat there.

"No," Hugh said, shaking his great head almost sadly. "Look, Miss Forrest, you will probably add 'insane' to your list of adjectives descriptive of me, but I must tell you this anyway. I had a dream about you *before* I saw you the first time—at the play."

Whack. Concussion. The blow of the flatiron sent my head flying across the room. Everything I had imagined was true, and for Hugh too. Sweet Christ.

"At the play?" I repeated, idiotically.

"In the first row that Sunday afternoon, when you made me lose my balance. I wanted to kill you," he said. He picked up a saltshaker and studied it. "I'm not sure I still don't."

"And the drawing?" I said, yet more stupidly than before.

"And the drawing made it clear to me that you had to be the woman in the first row. But the worst part of all was the dream."

"The dream," I repeated.

He did not appear to find my responses peculiar; I reminded myself he'd had a lot of experience with dialogue.

"The night of my birthday, the night before you came to see *The Lion's Share*, I had a strange dream. I dreamed I was up on the roof of a church—"

"The church in that film," I said.

He looked at me with the very same look he'd given me in the theater; again it made my spine explode. "The church in that film," he went on. "And I fell off the roof. . ."

"And landed on the lawn. . ."

"At your feet. And I looked up at you and. . ."

"Felt lonely." I didn't realize I was going to say it.

We stared at our plates. Hugh signaled for the waiter, who took away our untouched lunches, looking crestfallen. Hugh upended his bourbon into the glass of milk, downed most of it, offered me the rest (I drank it), took my hand, and headed for the door. All I allowed myself to think was that I was very hungry.

18. Leon

Possibly, I thought, I could learn to like Boston very much: it's a city of walkable size, smaller than London, but with the same civilized, historical air, and the feel of being a sensible place where actual people lead actual lives. I suppose that's rather ridiculous; one could say that my view of New York was warped by the fact that I'd only stayed in the best hotels and associated with the "upper classes" (America does have them, no matter what Americans say), and that might be true, but still, I liked what I'd seen of Boston. My memories of another visit, years before, had faded almost completely; that time our stay had been short and packed with tiring appointments. The hotel was very nice as well—not too big, not too ritzy (do pardon the pun), but dignified and extremely comfortable. I thought that if I ever really did take a vacation, I might come to Boston and really "do" the town.

Anyway, Hugh and I were able to establish ourselves at the Ritz-Carlton by ten o'clock in the morning, and I sent out for a wonderful breakfast of fresh fruit, cereal, and spinach-filled croissants. I ate like a starving soldier: I was nervous already—also, I wanted to play for time, keeping Hugh in the room and occupied as long as possible. He was not much interested in breakfast, however; he played with the fruit for a while, assembling a series of still-lifes along the mantelpiece, then drank two coffees, a glass of milk, and a shot of straight bourbon from a little airline bottle he'd secreted in his pocket. He then, for some reason, had me send his shoes out for a shine, although they were in perfect condition. While he waited for them to be returned, he put on his great floppy slippers (his are the largest feet of any man alive) and lay down on the bed.

"Leon," he said, "do you think me handsome?"

I looked at him with scorn. "Stop fishing for compliments."

"No, truly, Leon, what do you think?"

"I think you're bloody adorable," I said, winking at him.

He laughed. "Don't try to steal a kiss," he said, and threw a pillow at me.

I laughed as well. It was an in-joke for us, from back in our navy days, when Hugh had bewitched the hideous and vile-tempered company laundress into doing up his considerable civilian wardrobe as well as his uniforms, a thing she was strictly forbidden to do by naval regulations. One day, quite late in the game, it finally dawned upon her that she was being used, and after giving him a proper tongue-lashing, she turned upon him in her wrath and said, quite inanely, "I'm warning you, Mr. Sheenan. Don't try to steal a kiss." It became the byword of the entire company.

I wondered briefly if this would be one of Hugh's increasingly frequent fear-of-aging days, but the hotel man came back with the shoes very quickly, and soon Hugh was ready to be off. It was nearly eleven o'clock. He began pacing.

"I want to walk out in the sun," he said. "Let's hop it."

"Two things," I told him. "One, there is no sun—it's about to rain buckets. And two, you'll be much more noticeable here than you are in New York. I thought you wanted to keep this visit quiet?"

"Right as usual, old boy." He sat down again. "But what shall we do till one?"

I suggested a nap. My boiled-egg eyes were fast turning to stone.

"No," he said. "I want to *do* something. I wish to go shopping. I need a large hat. I really do, Leon; I have just the one in mind. But of course, you are right about going out now. I do not want to spend what's left of the morning being interviewed by some puppy from a college newspaper."

"What kind of hat do you need?" I asked, sensing an errand I might send myself on so I could see a bit of the city. If I couldn't take a nap, I'd as soon get out of the hotel. It was easy to see that Hugh was nervy about the luncheon with Miss Forrest and would probably become unbearable in a very short time.

He lay back down on the bed, with his big feet on the pillows and his head hanging down a bit over the foot. He looked like a freakishly large marionette.

"I'm thinking of a largish, soft, khaki-colored hat, with those little breathing-holes around the band, and I want the band to be brown and folded and on the thin side. Lots of stitching on the brim. No feathers or doodaddles. Rainproof, if possible. Able to be folded in the pocket. You know."

It didn't sound as though it would be too hard to find. "I remember where some of the shops are from our last visit," I lied, hoping that Hugh would believe my memory for such details could last so long. "Shall I go try to find you this hat?"

I know now that Hugh must have been making a mighty

effort to restrain his joy as I took his cunning bait and ran with it. "There's really no need to bother," he said nonchalantly, "if you'd rather stay here."

I told him I could use a breath of air, and as I took the lift down to street level I congratulated myself on my good fortune. I had made Hugh promise not to leave the suite before I returned, and he had done so with what seemed like sincere agreement, stating vehemently again that he did not wish to be "discovered." I told him I'd be back in good time to ready him for his engagement. As was my habit, I scoured the room for contraband bottles before I left, but found nothing. Hugh appeared to be falling asleep when I closed the door.

An hour and a half later, when I had become as thoroughly lost as Hugh must have known I would, I started to look for a cab. It had begun to rain quite hard. There were obviously only five or six cabs in the entire city of Boston, and these, when they did appear, ignored me with the greatest finesse. I asked directions of a policeman, who could not understand me, nor I him. He was speaking a Boston sort of English, I suppose, but I didn't get it. I walked back six blocks to the shop where I'd purchased Hugh's hat (I had found the perfect specimen, but only after trying a hundred places, though it was the kind of hat any respectable haberdasher in London would easily have been able to provide) and asked directions again, but this time I was given such a complicated set of instructions that my head began to ache in despair. A woman bystander suggested I take the "T," or subway, and unleashed upon me the scenario for yet another impossible journey. I could not abide the underground, in any case.

By the time I found my savior—in the guise of a hippie-ish looking young man selling newspapers on a street corner, who gave perfectly simple and lucid directions in understandable, well-chosen words—it was clear to me that I would be late for lunch. And that Hugh had certainly planned it that way. I started to walk.

As it happened, I was not really that far from the hotel, but by the time I found it, having circled and retraced my steps several times, it was a quarter after one. I was wet and angry and wanted nothing more than to repair to the suite for a wash and a change, but I was afraid I'd be needed in the dining room—though exactly for what I could not imagine. Hugh had made it plain that he did not want me to be present when Miss Forrest arrived, and while I could not really think what harm could come to either of them at a luncheon in a public dining room, a trusted little voice inside me told me I had to find them.

I deposited my jacket and the dripping shopping bag containing Hugh's hat at the coat-check and told the hostess in hushed tones that I'd like to have a drink at the bar before being seated a table. I chose a stool off to the darkest side of the bar, ordered some seltzer, and scanned the room by means of the large mirror facing me. I did not see Hugh at all at first, but then I noticed a long, ivory-colored leg extending out into the aisle near some gigantic plants. I moved a few seats to my left, and from there I was able to see them.

There sat Hugh, like a great doltish child, with his hands in his lap, and across from him (I could only see her back, which was absurdly straight, as if she were practicing some kind of yoga posture) sat the mysterious Miss Forrest—in a pale-yellow dress, just as she'd promised to wear. Their plates sat in front of them, apparently untouched, and they appeared to be speaking very little. Suddenly Hugh threw some bills on the table, snatched up the woman's hand, and propelled her out the door of the restaurant with breathtaking speed.

My impulse, of course, was to follow, and so I did. Hugh left Miss F. in the foyer, fairly vaulted into a waiting lift, and was down again in a flash carrying his trench coat, my trench coat (I assumed for her), and a hat exactly like the one I had purchased a few hours earlier. Somehow, I reasoned, he'd taken possession of this hat within the last couple of days, and its description had popped into his mind when he was searching for an errand that would take me out of his way that morning. It was irritating, to say the least, but by that time I was too intrigued by the little drama opening before me to pay my irritation much mind. Hugh helped Miss F. into my coat (it did not do wonders for her), donned his own, bringing the collar well up around his face, pulled his blasted hat down as far as it would go, and left by the side door, arm in arm with his companion. It looked as if they were heading for the park, and I only hoped they would not step into the car we had hired, which was waiting at the curb outside the hotel. I wanted to shadow them at my leisure.

19. Nora

"Put this on," said Hugh, wrapping me in a man's raincoat that was, shall we say, a bit roomy, and at the same time stuffing his arms into an old battered trench I assumed was his own. The coat I was wearing could not possibly have been his: it was obviously meant for a much heavier man and came several inches below my knees—anything of Hugh's would have dragged along the floor. He also produced a floppy sort of safari hat, tugged it down over his ears, and flipped up his coat collar all around so that only a bit of his face was showing.

He looked me over and laughed. "Perfect," he said. "Smashing." He took my arm and steered me out the Arlington Street door, rushing me past the elderly doorman as if we were being chased by the hound of heaven.

When Hugh had gone upstairs a few minutes before, "to fetch some things," I'd stood in the lobby of the Ritz-Carlton in a state of perfect calm—or perfect insanity. I cannot say which. Standing there waiting for Hugh Sheenan did not seem like an abnormal thing to be doing. I did not feel nervous or upset at all. The conversation we'd had over the lunch we hadn't eaten had shocked me while it was happening, but once what I privately referred to as "the thing" had been stated I'd felt the worst to be over. We were on equal terms at last; we both knew the score. And though neither of us understood what was happening—had been happening—to us, we were like two people on a scavenger hunt, both determined to gain possession of the same peculiar treasure and both in the grip of a manic and party-like mood.

Even my embarrassment and my million insecurities seemed to have vanished. Although I had tried all day not to dwell on my appearance (which failed to reach anything remotely close to perfection, even on my best days), my first exposure to Hugh in the dining room had plunged me into an immediate depression. Next to him, I looked like what my mother would have called "something the cat dragged in." I knew it shouldn't matter, but it did. His charismatic presence was stupefying, and part of the anguish that had provoked me into tears so early in the conversation was probably simply that I felt so physically unworthy to be sitting there.

I did not feel that way anymore, and it was glorious. I felt light and confident—like someone else, I thought, some happily unself-conscious being. I was afraid only that someone would recognize Hugh and force us to leave the small world we'd begun to create, even for a minute. As soon as he returned and put on his hat and coat I felt better: the only really noticeable thing about him then was his height, and people in Boston were not accustomed to scouting for celebrities anyway. Also, his being with me, an average-looking woman in a plain coat, made him less remarkable still. With any luck, I figured, we'd be left alone.

We crossed Arlington Street and entered the Public Garden through one of the side gates, cut across the soggy grass, and started along one of the paths that traces the edge of the pond. Although the rain that had started while we were in the restaurant had all but ceased, there were only a few people about: some elderly Chinese people engaged in hypnotic tai chi, a few teenagers searching the trash bins for soda cans, the occasional mother and child-in-stroller.Nobody looked twice at us. Hugh was striding along at a terrible pace. I pulled on his arm.

"Wait up," I said. "Where's the fire?"

He stopped dead, looked at me, and laughed. "So sorry," he said. "I don't even know where we're going. What is this place?"

"This is the part of the Boston Common called the Public Garden," I told him. "If we take this path"—I pointed away from the pond—"it might be a little more private."

"Just the ticket," he said, and we walked that way, more slowly than before. Eventually, in fact, we slowed almost to a stop.

"Miss Forrest," Hugh said. "I find myself in a most unusual state: at a loss for words."

"You'd better call me Nora."

"And you'd better call me. . . something. You've yet to use my name. How about 'You Old Fool'?"

"Hugh."

"Good. Nora, we seem quite safe here."

I looked around. A gentle fog had descended. We were approaching a corner of the park, surrounded by dripping pine trees, that looked, in the misty afternoon light, like the one place in the world I'd always wanted to be. There was a long bench with a broken seat, and we went and sat upon it after Hugh made a huge show of wiping it down with his blue handkerchief, which he then held up to me, sopping wet. "No more weeping," he said. "We have nothing with which to staunch the flow of waters." He squeezed it out, wadded it up, and tossed it into a barrel.

We sat about a foot and a half apart, turned toward each other. I still felt perfectly at ease, but my mind was as blank as a bathtub. I waited for him to speak—or not speak. I felt I could wait there all my life, perfectly content. Dim memories of my "real" life seemed to stand outside the park gates, looking in wistfully, like orphans outside a rich kid's yard viewing a birthday party—a party complete with a delicious pony. A faint consciousness of city noises hovered behind me somewhere, just barely keeping me pinned to a material existence. But I still felt so hungry that my stomach betrayed me and growled.

20. Rick

I stayed out late with Emil and Jack that night not because I was having an especially good time, but because I had picked up an unspoken message from Nora that she wanted to be alone. Maybe she didn't know it herself, but I did. Things had been going very well for us ever since what I found myself calling her "recovery," and I didn't want to push my luck. She'd left me once, before we were married, because I'd fairly forced her to go—forced her by not stopping her from leaving—and when we'd gotten back together, some five years ago, I'd promised myself that I'd never let her go again. That is not to say that everything was perfect; when is it ever, and who would expect it to be? But I respected her silences, and her separateness, too much now to underestimate them. She, in her turn, trusted me with them, and that was a gift in and of itself. Nora is the kind who will give and give and give—of her own accord—and who only really desires not to be asked to give that most precious of gifts: an explanation of herself.

It's true that men don't talk to each other much—straight men, anyway. At least that's what I've observed. Oh, I mean, men talk, but they don't say much about their feelings or relationships—that's common knowledge, and true. Men gossip in their own way, but they draw the line much earlier than women do. When something really awful happens, and letting their friends know about it is unavoidable, men stick to the facts. Their buddies listen and shake their heads and offer a few well-meant but trite condolences or commiserations. A lot of back slapping goes on. Rarely does advice rear its ugly head, and women find that hard to understand. I'm generalizing, of course, but still, on the whole, it's all true. And as I sat in Barney's with Jack and Emil, two dear old friends for whom I'd easily give an arm and a leg, I felt for once so bogged down in their inarticulate camaraderie I was close to screaming. It was just one of those nights; there was nothing particularly wrong, but I missed my Nora. I wanted to hold her in my arms and lie on our old couch in the moonlight with some kind of wordless music on the stereo and listen to her talk and talk and talk. I wanted to talk to her too. I wanted to tell her all the things I'd never told her, to open my soul to her and have her neaten it up, the way the mother did to the children's minds in *Peter Pan* when she sorted out all their thoughts and dreams. It was a crazy kind of night; I remember wondering if there was a full moon or something.

Emil and Jack were dawdling over their beers, making stupid jokes, and generally driving me nuts. We'd been to a Red Sox game, and all they could talk about was Wade Boggs's batting average and how many points up and down it had gone in the past two weeks. I wished I'd gone to the game with Nora; she knew all Boggs's numbers too, but she also would have been talking about his new beard, and about the way the lights at Fenway made the infield grass look blue, and about some person in the bleachers who'd caught her eye, and a lot of other things. If I'd taken Nora to the game, I'd be home right now waiting for her to brush her teeth and come to bed. I left my boys and went home on the T, pleading an early morning the next day and trying to take their head shaking and back slaps with good humor.

All the way home I thought of Nora, wondering what she'd done with her friend all day and what kind of mood she'd be in when I finally saw her. It was pretty late, but she might still be awake. A day with Mellie usually filled her up with all sorts of stories and observations and news, and I was looking forward to hearing about it, though I didn't really care about any of that stuff; I just had this big desire to hear Nora's voice.

But when I got home she was already asleep. She'd left me a note saying she was exhausted and she hoped I'd had a good time at the game. Bummer. But I didn't want to wake her up.

As I turned out the lights in the kitchen I noticed the little answering machine light was blinking away, so I pushed the "message" button. Nora's voice, sounding a bit remote, said, "Hi Rick. I'm staying to dinner at Mellie's. I might be a little late. Hope you had a good day. See you later." I wondered what time she'd left the message, then realized she must have come home early after all and forgotten to erase it.

I turned on the light in the bathroom, which partly illuminated the bed if you positioned the door just right, and went in to look at Nora. When I saw her sleeping I knew her note hadn't lied: she really did look exhausted; she almost looked sick. Her face was clenched instead of relaxed, and her hair was all damp and stuck to her forehead. I smoothed the hair away and kissed her nose. She stirred a little, and turned her head. I thought she mumbled something about a flower, but I couldn't really understand her.

21. Nora

"Oh gaaawd," Hugh said when he heard my rumbling innards. "We never did manage anything to eat, did we, my dear?" He looked aghast at his failure as a gentleman to provide a lady with nourishment.

I laughed. "I don't really feel like eating," I said. "But I do seem to need something solid in here." I patted my stomach.

"I could use something solid myself," he said, "but where do we go?"

I looked over the iron fences, foolishly; I knew there was nothing in the neighborhood but a fancy bar on Boylston and the trendy Newbury Street eateries, where I was sure Hugh would be recognized. I might even meet someone I know, I thought for the first time—I did occasionally run into acquaintances in Boston. It astonished me that I hadn't thought of that before; it would spell disaster. I imagined someone mentioning it to Rick, sometime before I'd gotten up the nerve to tell him. "Boy oh boy," the person would say, "you could have knocked me over with a feather when I saw old Nora walk into Joe's on the arm of that movie star." Life would just be over.

Hugh tapped my shoulder. "Penny for your thoughts," he said. I must have been musing too long.

"Hugh, I'd really rather not leave here. I mean, it's so lovely, and there's no one around. . ."

"Who might know you?"

"Yes," I admitted.

There was a long pause. And then, "Are you married, Nora?"

"Yes." I took a long breath. "His name is Rick."

Hugh smiled ruefully. "And does he know where you went today?"

I looked him straight in the eye. "No, he doesn't."

"Why is that?"

I wondered if he could be making fun of me. "Because, in a way, I didn't know where I was going. I didn't know what would happen—it didn't have anything to do with him." I looked at Hugh. "And I wish you hadn't brought it up."

He picked up my hand and turned it over, palm up, and kissed it. A huge peony opened in my chest.

"Don't worry," he said. "I didn't know where I was going myself. I don't think I do even now." We sat then a while, just loosely holding hands. I think we were waiting for our last words to wash away in the dripping fog. I felt weightless, unmoored. I sailed away from myself.

After a while Hugh broke the silence. "When I was younger, Nora," he said, "I believed in a lot of things. I believed in God—oh, how I believed in him!—and in honor and freedom, and socialism. . . and much, much more." He let go of my hand and pulled his coat tightly around himself, as if he'd suddenly grown very cold. "And I didn't believe in any sort of 'silliness'—no conspiracy theories, or tarot cards, or space ships from Mars, or horoscopes, or psychologists. . . or dreams. The one thing I believed in always—and more than anything else—was art. Can you understand that, Nora?"

"Very well," I said.

"And now that I'm old. . ."

"Not old," I said—predictably, but sincerely. He was ageless to me, and ageless, I suspected, to himself.

"Older, then, thank you," he continued, picking up my hand again. "Now that I'm older I have art only. No wife, no lovers of import. A child I hardly see. No politics to speak of, no God to censure me. I sometimes think I'm like a slug: no apparent inner or outer structure. But Nora, I have my art. I could not bear for that to desert me. I tell myself I have some good years left with it, but who knows? And you have your drawing, so you can understand that. You may not be famous. But you have. . . powers." He stopped and looked over my shoulder and in the strange, pale light of the fog I examined his face: I saw the deep, raked lines around his eyes and mouth, the imperfections of his skin, the growth of grey-black beard beginning to show along his jaw. I saw him flawed, and plainly. As he spoke I kept my eyes on his wide mouth and his fairly unattractive teeth, and on the way he paused between phrases, with his mouth partly open and his tongue resting lazily just inside his lower lip. I told myself I did not like it. Although his words thrilled me, they were like a just-sharpened knife: gleaming and seductive. I think I was trying to hate him.

"What I mean is," he went on, "when I had that dream about you, and then saw you in the theater that afternoon, I can tell you I didn't feel too cocky. And when I saw your drawing, saw into your drawing, I should say, I was felled like an unsuspecting, stupid, bloody oak."

"I never meant to—"

"No. No, I know you meant no harm. I don't think anymore, now that I've met you, that it was anything you controlled." He grinned. "I no longer think that you're a witch, though I admit that for a while I did think so. I don't know who or what designed all this—I can't imagine. I only know that you and I are the only ones who know it happened—whatever it was—and that you're the only one I can discuss it with, remember it with. The only one. . . But I must tell you, Nora, how angry I was with you. I blamed you for all my fears—so awfully unfair, isn't it?" He shook his head. "That afternoon in the theater, as I told you at lunch, I wanted to kill you. I think I might have done, if I'd had the chance. It was irrational. It wasn't just that you'd thrown me off balance with your stare. It wasn't just that. I was scared silly, I thought I was losing my mind. I thought—felt very strongly—that I was in danger of never being able to give a decent performance again, that art had been drained from my veins by a vampire: you, Nora. You. I began to be afraid I'd look for you everywhere, in every audience—see you everywhere. And the worst part was, I wanted to. I wanted to see you, Nora, old thing, and never more so than when I received your drawing."

"I don't know why I sent it," I told him. "I don't even know how I drew it, really. It just. . . came about."

I told him pretty much everything then—from before the play to the night I drew the picture—and he listened very carefully and seriously to all of it, with his great head bowed. Sometimes he would look up at me, searching my face intensely. I did not feel ashamed to admit anything to him; it all seemed impersonal, it seemed as though I were talking about two other people. I had never spoken that way to anyone before, not even in the confessional. It felt as if we were detectives discussing a case, so that we could find a clue that might explain the things that had happened.

We talked a long while; it was growing dark. I knew I had to leave, but I couldn't until we'd found some kind of answer. And yet I suspected there was no answer to find. We talked in ever-diminishing circles, but we could never find the center of the thing, and that is why we loved it, and why we finally stopped talking.

With arms linked, we walked back around the pond, very slowly. It was warm and the thick fog had enveloped the gardens; we opened our coats. He took off the hat and stuffed it in his pocket; it had made a little ridge around his hair that I wanted to touch. He walked me slowly over to a tree and leaned me up against it. Of course he kissed me.

He began as slowly as we'd been walking, kissing me gently around my mouth, then on it, licking my lips tentatively, but never putting his tongue inside. Neither of us closed our eyes at first, as if we wanted to be sure we were awake. We kissed for a very long time, still holding hands. He tasted of cigarettes and salt and milky bourbon.

I kissed him back the way he kissed me, as if we had all the time in the world—as if there were no time or world. We kissed and we kissed and there was fog on our faces, then finally Hugh pulled me into his coat and I felt his hardness. It did not startle me. I was not Nora Forrest. I wanted him so badly then that I would have let him take me against the tree, or on the wet path. I thought I would fall down, but he held me up and held me.

After a minute or two of that, Hugh pulled back slowly and led me to a bench. He sat me down on one end of it, then sat himself a foot or two away. "Hold on," he said, smiling. "Let us just hold on a moment or two."

I laughed. I tried to catch my breath, which seemed to

be coming visibly, in little cartoon clouds; I felt as if I'd taken some psychedelic drug.

"Dearheart," Hugh said, and laughed in an astonished way. We both laughed. We talked about the pigeons and the mallards on the pond, and finally he looked straight into me and said, "Let's go now."

"All right," I said. "I will have to make a call."

He didn't answer, only put his hat back on and pulled up the collar of his coat. We went back to the hotel and he took me to a corner of the lobby, where a public telephone was housed in a plush little booth. He vanished around the corner.

I called home. Rick was out—I'd forgotten he was going to a ballgame. The answering machine picked up.

"Hi, Rick," somebody's voice said into it, "I'm staying to dinner at Mellie's. I might be a little late. Hope you had a good day. See you later."

When I came out, Hugh met me. We went upstairs.

22. Leon

I could tell right away I needn't fear Hugh would realize he was being followed. He was obviously so wrapped up in Miss F. that he saw nothing else. The two of them walked closely together, deep in conversation I suppose, and at first they walked so quickly I had trouble keeping up.

I'd already been walking around all day and I was hungry and tired. But finally they slowed down, and eventually came to a stop on a bench in a corner of the gardens where the evergreens were lush and I could easily find a hiding place. It was very wet, though. The day had not shaped up to be one of my favorites, and I thought back wistfully to that morning in the hotel, when I'd happily planned to visit this city again on my own. Now I was thinking twice about that. But I told myself, sensibly, that nothing really terrible had happened, that it was only another of Hugh's little escapades, and that because these capers had been less and less frequent in recent years, I'd become ill-accustomed to dealing with them.

The air was so sodden and the place so deserted I could hear Hugh and Miss F. quite clearly, though I had taken up a post behind some shrubbery about twenty-five feet away. I could hear them easily enough, but I did not understand them. The more I listened, the more confused I became. I had been correct in assuming that this whole mystery revolved around the drawing, but now I was hearing that there were connections to the dream Hugh had told me and the woman he'd seen at the play. Quite preposterously, I thought, he seemed to be connecting all three.Miss F. went along with him in this and spoke to him comfortably, as if she'd known him a very long time. She told him silly things about herself, which I put down to ingenuousness and hero-worship, but which Hugh accepted easily, as if she were the oldest of friends. What was this? Who was this young woman? Had Hugh a secret life, of which I knew nothing? It was not possible; we were together more than most married couples, had been so for so many years. My mind did drift off and perhaps I missed a few things, but all in all I could make neither head nor tail of what they were saying.

At last the seduction began, and that I understood. I had seen Hugh kiss the palms of countless ladies. I knew just the way he took hold of their elbows and steered them around, his height, his long stride, and his imposing presence rendering them creatures fully under his control. I had studied the way he riveted them with his practiced eyes, exposed their secrets, received their confessions like a tender, avuncular priest, scooped out their inhibitions, tossed them away, and began to kiss those eager, upturned faces. Once, in the early days of Maryann's reign, I had even seen him making love, though he didn't know it. She and Hugh had rushed headlong into his bedroom while I was putting things away in the walk-in closet, and I, to my dishonor, had not made myself known. Instead,

I'd watched from behind the half-closed door as if watching a film—but only for a half-minute. I felt embarrassed for Maryann's sake. Oh, she was smooth and beautiful—but I was not titillated. Maybe I thought there would be something different about what Hugh did in bed, or the way he did it. I suppose in an odd way I just wanted to know everything about him, like a parent. But he seemed to do the deed like other men, or even a little more clumsily. Uncovered, and in motion, his interminable legs and arms seemed ungainly and bizarre.

At any rate, as the Americans say, I knew all his moves. When he kissed Miss F's cupped palm I thought to myself, so that's it: all this dramatic folderol and hide-and-seek for a bit of silly sex. Perhaps he needed more drama surrounding the thing now than he had done in his younger days—*That must be it*, I thought. There had not been any women in a while, and although I could not instantly see what was so exciting about this rather odd-looking, smallish person, I simply thought, *To each his own*. I did not care.

Moisture from my collar had begun to run down my back—remember, I did not have my coat. I wanted him to get on with it. I wanted him to bed her in a hurry (or in as much of a hurry as his heart could stand) and send her swiftly home so we could get back to New York. I prayed she would be a one-nighter and not encumber us with another set of American-female woes.

At last they began to move, walking toward the pond (and, I hoped, the hotel, though again my sense of direction had betrayed me), and again they started off quickly and gradually slowed down. Hugh steered her to a tree, gently pushed her up against it, and began to kiss her. It looked uncomfortable. I moved in closer. Then I saw Hugh's face and I felt the shame I had not felt that day I watched him from the closet. He kissed Miss F. with his eyes open, and they were his true eyes, not his stagey, manipulative ones. He was baring his soul to this girl-woman, and he thought she was the only one to see.

Her eyes were open as well, and as naked as his were. I turned away. I felt stupid and ill and revolted. I knew I should not have been there.

And after an endless time, while I stared at my rain-soaked shoes, they repaired to a park bench, laughing. Laughing. I could not hear them anymore and I did not want to. When they got up I walked behind them until they entered the hotel and then I thought, *I'll go have a bit of dinner, I'll go to a film, maybe two films.* My job was over for the evening; Hugh was on his own.

I walked down some street until I found a little shop where I bought a sack of chocolate biscuits and a newspaper. I wanted to go to a film that lacked romance, but I feared I would have trouble finding such a thing.

23. Hugh

At the moment I first held Nora Forrest in my arms, I thought of that cat, Horatio. When Leon and I had last gone back to England, I had somehow forgotten about Horatio for days, and yet one morning I woke and suddenly noticed him there in the room with me, languidly basking in the sunlight on top of a sweater I'd thrown on the window seat the night before. *My God*, I thought, *he's been here always, silently waiting, intimate and aloof and self-satisfied all at the same time, as only a cat can be*. He'd had no need to announce himself, I thought—how admirable. Probably he'd lived at my house long before I even knew he'd existed.

Nora felt like a cat, all nerves and bones and hesitancy, until she relaxed. Then I felt her whole body loosen, as if she'd become pure silk. When I pulled her inside my coat she seemed to melt into me, and the desire I felt for her at that moment shook me awake from a lifetime of sleepier yearnings. Far from wanting to kill her, I now wanted to rend my body apart at the breastbone and pull her deeper and deeper into my very blood and core. I suppose it was a female impulse, drawn from some primitive place one seldom likes to go. My other impulses were entirely male, however; I thought my body would burst apart with its compulsion to possess her. I had to stop kissing her, holding her, drinking her in. It was either that or take her instantly, standing up against the tree or lying on the sodden path. Ridiculous.

When we stopped kissing, I guided her to a bench and placed her a little away from me. We were both giddy—like teenagers whose experimentation had gotten quite away from them. I lit a cigarette. Nora asked me for one. I was surprised to see her begin to smoke like a veteran, but the Galoises proved too strong for her, and she soon let the cigarette drop to the wet ground, unnecessarily stamping it down with her foot.

It was then I noticed her yellow stockings. Her skirt was on the long side, and Leon's coat had hidden much of the rest of her legs. I reached over and moved the layers of cloth just up to her knee, running my hand along her calf as I did so. Yes, her hose were the palest yellow.

She shivered perceptibly when I touched her. She smiled. "You're not helping me calm down," she said.

"I just noticed your stockings," I said, moronically. "They're yellow."

"Yes," she said. "To match the dress I bought for the play."

"I did think it was the same one."

"Yes."

I looked up at her, keeping my palm on her leg. "You're the color of a beam of light."

She flushed a little. After all that had happened that day, that one statement made her blush. She was a funny witch; I was enchanted.

"Nora," I continued, feeding on her bashfulness, "you're like a gillyflower."

"What's that?" she asked me, smiling. She was radiant—an opal, a vamp, a duckling. I could not put a description to her, but I was helpless to do anything but touch her. I held her hand and looked out over what was left of the world in the fog and deepening light.

"When I was a child in Ireland," I told her, "every now and then my brothers and I would find a kind of small carnation on the cliffs, growing close to the ground. We knew our mother loved them. She called them gillyflowers. And whenever we'd bring her one she'd take it lovingly in her hands and say, 'You really oughtn't pluck them up, you know—there are so few—but I do love having them about the house for as long as they last.' And she'd put the flower in a blue glass vase and set it on the windowsill over her desk in the sunlight. 'I always say,' she'd tell us, all smiling, 'the good Lord always sends me a gillyflower when I need one.' And she'd give us a kiss and a pat on the arse and send us back out to play." To cover my sudden emotion, I added, "The silly things were usually dead by morning."

"What a beautiful story," she said, looking pensive and more flowerlike than ever.

"And they were the palest yellow, just like you."

"Mr. Sheenan, you're turning my head," she teased.

"My silly little gillyflower," I said, looking far into her eyes (as usual, I found no end to them). "We can go now."

As we walked arm in arm back to the hotel, we did not speak. I was thinking of a number of practical matters. I knew she had to make her telephone call, and I was trying to remember where the booth was in the lobby—I knew I had seen one. I didn't want her making a call from my room; I didn't want to hear her. Also, while putting on my hat, I had noticed that wretched Leon skulking in the park, just beyond us. I wondered what he had seen and heard. *Well, bugger him*, I thought. Walking with Nora I felt, for the first time in years, a feeling I'd forgotten: the feeling of being just one of a million-million human beings. I had no fear of being recognized, or any desire to be, which was always the other side of the coin. She had thrown a shawl of protection about me and I would not let Leon's presence wrench it away. Besides, he did have his discretion; he was no Peeping Tom. I knew once he realized where we were headed he would soon leave us alone.

Nora made her call. She came out of the little telephone-room looking serious but composed, and I thought, good, no hysterics. I had to admit to myself I was afraid she'd leave right then—that she'd phoned from our world to the one from whence she'd come, and been summoned back by a heartless black magic. You are truly a blasted old fool, I thought, you are dotty. We went upstairs.

In the lift the operator smiled at us and said, "Nasty weather," giving our wrinkled, saturated coats the once-over.

"To the contrary, my good man," I said, "this New England mist reminds me fondly of home."

The man smiled again, too well trained to take it further. It made me feel quite possessive; I felt I belonged there with Nora, that we were just an ordinary couple who'd been out enjoying the town.

I unlocked the suite and ushered Nora in. I turned on some small lamps and lifted Leon's coat from her shoulders. She trembled.

"You've caught a chill," I said. "Some brandy?"

She did not answer me, but I poured some for each of us from the bottle I'd smuggled in past poor old Leon. She went and curled up on the sofa with her glass, looking down into it and not at me. I wanted to go to her, to hold her against me again, but I kept away, remembering Horatio.

Finally, she said, "I am cold, I guess."

It was warm in the room—I had just been considering letting in some air—so I knew her condition was not a physical one. She was all nerved up, she needed uncoiling. I wondered when she would ever let me touch her, though I did not doubt that she would, eventually. I sat down opposite her in a chair, thinking how to gentle her out of her mood. "It must have been the fog," I said. "Perhaps a warm bath?"

There was a short pause, and I thought I'd said the wrong thing—then, "Bawth?" she repeated, in my accent. She smiled hugely, suddenly all aglow. I could not believe my luck: she wanted to have a bath with me!

I smiled back, restraining my desire to lift her up and carry her off like a bandit. "Shall I run the water?"

She nodded, and I bolted for the bathroom door. I found some scented bath salts in the cabinet that Leon must have intended for my pacification (amazing what that man will pack for a one-night stay) and dumped them into the tub. I turned on the taps and let steaming water rush over them; it smelled wonderful, like a forest of pines. I checked the towels, which were in good supply and fluffy. Then I went out and fetched Nora, who'd already shed her sandals, and led her, shoes and brandy glass in hand, to the edge of the magical waters.

She breathed in deeply and said, "Heaven. Thank you, Hugh."

And then, before I realized what she was doing, she gently pushed me out and closed the door.

24. Nora

I knew of no precedent for any of this; I had nothing to take my cue from, nothing in my experience, nothing I'd seen in print. I don't know who the woman was who closed Hugh out of the bathroom—she did it so smoothly, so unexpectedly, I was filled with surprise and admiration for her. I saw him as she closed the door; he looked both surprised and reverent. Then she closed the lid of the john and sat down. Eventually she reached over and turned off the taps, just before the water would have sloshed over the edge and soaked the cream-colored rug. She set down the glass of brandy, and then she began, very quietly, to cry.

She cried for me, I think, but not entirely in sorrow, and not for long. She opened the john and peed, then washed her hands, splashed water on her face, and looked around. Some of Hugh's things were set out on the counter: a brush and comb, some lavender-scented shaving cream, Mylanta, aspirin, a straightedge razor. She tested the edge of the razor's blade on the back of her hand and quickly put it down. She ran her fingers through the brush and drew out some short black hairs, some grey and brown ones too.

Holding these up to the light, she examined them closely, looking for God knows what. I thought she'd probably put them somewhere, as a keepsake, but she scattered them over the rug, like ashes or crumbs.

This is a fortunate woman, I thought. I longed to see her enter her bath, her luxurious preparation for a night of passion. She was so single-minded, so self-confident. I pictured her slipping her soft, loose dress over her head, revealing her fortunate body. She'd remove the pale yellow stockings slowly, seductively, as if Hugh were still there. This was a woman capable of patience and subtle allure: she had postponed her fondest desire, only to make it fonder still.

I don't know how long she stood there, watching Hugh's hairs drift from her fingers endlessly through time and shadow—it seemed to take an age. She appeared to know I was there, but she did not care that I watched her. The room was swollen with steam and the scent of fir trees. I suddenly knew that something dreadful was happening, that a choice was being made for me as irrevocably as choices are made for us before birth by our parents' bodies. This would be something I'd have to "live with, make the best of, learn to cope with." I could not move for grief. Languidly, with a look of resignation, the woman finally reached out her hand to me, and I stepped inside her.

I found her body uncomfortable at first: it seemed a little drunk, a little cruel. I tried to take her dress off, to defy her and step into the bath, but her fingers would not work. Her hands were unsteady, and had somehow become cold and stiff in the steamy room. I sat in this second-hand body, on the soft, damp rug, until gradually I took it over completely.

I knew the woman had done me a favor, had given me the gift of her very life, but I could not forgive her. I thought of all the pleasure, the sweet pain, she would have found in Hugh's arms, and how I would have watched them happily, jealously, recording each movement and stillness, each murmur and silence, in the scrupulous record I'd been keeping of her life. What good had her sacrifice been to either of us? She was, for all purposes, dead now, and I lacked all her resources with which to carry on.

As swiftly, as surprisingly, as Hugh had been brought into my life, he had been suddenly torn away. Like his arrival, his departure was out of my control, but this time there was no dream, and no hope of one. By consenting to touch his real face, I had given up claim to the face that had possessed me for so long. I wanted to blame him; I knew I would blame him. But I also called him innocent in the caverns of my best heart.

I thought of what was lost, but not of what would happen. I did not think about Rick, about right or wrong, or even about the way that woman's body, now completely mine, ached inconceivably for the touch of a long-boned hand, the kiss of a too-wide, tender mouth, and the final, self-annihilating fulfillment.

I put on my shoes quite suddenly, as if someone had commanded me to do so, and stood by the door.

25. Hugh

Nora stayed in the bathroom a very long time, and the water ran so long and hard that I expected at any moment to see it gush from beneath the door. Finally, the water noises stopped, and there was silence for quite a while. I'd taken off my clothes and put on a poufy, hooded (Why were these bloody things always hooded? What dodo would wear a hood in the house?) hotel robe, deep red, with a white rope around the waist. Too short for me, of course. Checking myself in the mirror, I saw a tall, skinny, monkish-looking person with knobbly knees and an absurd grin on his face. I went and lay across the bed.

"Women are most hilarious," I prattled to myself, "experts in postponing satisfaction. They would rather primp and fuss for hours than get right to the heart of the matter." I laughed. I had another brandy. My stomach was fine. My heart was pumping like a locomotive. I was eighteen years old.

But as time dragged on, I began to feel uneasy. I went and knocked on the bathroom door. "Nora," I called out, "is everything fine in there?"

She did not answer but opened the door immediately, as if she'd been standing right behind. She was fully dressed; she'd even put her shoes back on. The tub was full to the brim with untouched water, not a bubble disturbed. The towels were still neatly folded. She walked briskly past me.

"What is it, my dear?" I asked, going to her and folding her in my arms. They were trembling.

She let me hold her, but she was limp and far away. I let her go.

I had a flash: perhaps she knew of my heart condition and had been worrying herself about endangering my life by making love. I rushed to reassure her. "Nora," I said, "if you're concerned about my health, please don't be. The doctors tell me there's absolutely no danger. . ."

That was not it at all; I could tell by her expression. "Hugh, I'm sorry," she said, "I'm sorry. . ." She looked at me with terrible eyes; she was crying. "I can't believe this, I can't help it, I can't tell you, I don't know what to say." She crumpled onto a chair and hid her face from me.

I knelt beside her and lifted her face up. I knew then all the meaning of the phrase "sick at heart." I was old again, I was grieving, I was alone. But I could not feel angry with her, I knew I'd try to help her. I smoothed her face with my shaky fingers and dried her eyes and said to her, "Tell me."

She got up then and began to walk about, touching anything in the room that was obviously mine. From an open valise she lifted a pair of blue gloves. She smiled inside her tears, gave me a sheepish look, folded them, and put them in her pocket. Then she came to me—I was still kneeling by the chair—and drew my head to her breast, stroking my hair.

I put my arms around her hips, but loosely. There was no passion in either of us at that moment; it was as if something—someone—had broken in and stolen it away.

"Hugh," she spoke softly into my hair, "I wanted you today more than I wanted to breathe. It was a feeling more pressing than anything—and more. . . part of me. . . than I can explain. It made me forget who I was, what my life was, who I lived with. I really didn't care. With all my heart I consented to come back here with you and make love all night and forever and blot out the world for as long as I could." She paused. "But I can't now. There's nothing I can do. Maybe I'm sick; I feel like someone else. The spell was broken somehow." She looked at me with a sickening, killing candor. "We should have done it in the park."

I was accustomed to hearing frank talk from women, but that statement really shocked me; my little hillside flower had dealt me a direct blow to the balls.

"Nora," was all I could muster.

She started pacing the room again, this time looking for her bag. "I have to go now. I have to. I cannot stand this." Her voice had risen to an alarming pitch; I thought she might be about to faint.

I started toward her. "Nora, what have I done to you? What have I done?" I asked her. I put my arms around her and she held me very close.

She said, still weeping, "You haven't done anything wrong. I'd give my life for another day like this, even though it hurts like hell." She drew back a little and looked up at me. "But Hugh," she said, "now I'm the one who's angry."

"Angry, dearheart?"

She stroked my face. We kissed then, one last time—the effect, at least on me, as devastating as the first time. But Nora broke away and stood by the door.

"Angry," she said, as she opened it and walked through. "You had," she said, "no right to become more than a dream for me." She gave me her first-row stare, which lopped off my head from my neck as neatly as a hatchet would. She closed the door.

After she left, I got into the bath, which was still lukewarm, and full to the top of the tub. Since I had not bothered to open the drain, my body displaced a great deal of water, which spilled out onto the carpet and floor. I just looked at it, feeling nothing, watching it slop over the doorsill.

I floated there for some time, possibly hours, until the skin on my elbows, fingertips, and heels could be rubbed off like so much dust—I was way beyond the puckering stage. My mind remained utterly blank throughout. Eventually, realizing I would certainly soon dissolve completely, I stepped out and donned the big red robe. I put the hood up. I sloshed through the bathroom swamp and went out to lie on the bed, taking with me a large glass of brandy, the bottle it came from, and my cigarettes.

I'd had nothing to eat since that absurd breakfast with Leon, and I was glad: I intended to get quite horribly drunk. I intended to get sick and old and die all at once that night, and have Leon find me, whenever he returned, not suffering from an evening of passion and play but stone-cold dead, and naked. Poor Leon. . . but I'd left him a mint in my will.

I took off the robe and got under the covers. I closed my eyes. The brandy was already doing its dastardly work, for with the greatest clarity I could see Nora, as she'd stood against that tree by the pond, and with agony I realized that a mere alcohol-induced vision of her could ruin me. I opened my eyes, sat up, and waited. I was feeling sick and did not like it, so I decided to eat something after all; I was still willing to die, but not before figuring a few things out.

I got up, unsteadily. Leon always kept a little stash of goodies in his kit bag, and there I found some bland English biscuits, a bag of unsalted peanuts, and some yellow apples. I threw the apples into the fireplace; I'm not sure why. Then I got back into bed with my booty and ate every last crumb and nut, washing it down with brandy and water. It was a beastly dinner, but it brought me a little to life.

One thing I knew was that I dared not close my eyes, so I sat up and smoked and thought about Nora. Was this all-consuming desire really the making of a few hours in a strange city with a strange woman who'd somehow bewitched me? It made no sense. Why had she touched me so? Did "God" do it? Was life at last revealing itself to me as a series of meaningless accidents? Was it just sex at the bottom of this deep and murky barrel, all the more insidious for its unexplainable presence? I thought not. For one thing, physically, Nora was not my type. When I first held her, I knew that, though it didn't mean a thing at the time. I have always been attracted to larger, darker, more luxuriously favored women; Nora's body was as firm as a boy's, and her breasts were small. Her face was mad-making—one moment soft and feminine, the next all muddled like a child's, and the next as firmly set as Leon's when he was scolding. She did have fantastic eyes, the irises a mixture of colors with gold toward the center and blues and greens along the outside, and all her considerable powers were vested there, in spades. But had I simply seen her on the street, I would not, I know, have looked twice.

There was no denying, however, how completely I had fallen for her, how the need had sprung up even before we kissed. I suppose it was while we were talking in the park that

I really fell, while we walked and talked in circles about the "coincidences" of the dream, the play, and her picture. We were like two souls removed from time, cast out on some damp and foggy planet to question the universe—its possibilities and its terrible rules. Talking with her then had given me the same feeling I'd had when our eyes locked in the theater that day, only without the fury. Our discussion—our every attention—was so focused on ourselves and our mysteries that there was nothing to do but dream we might—for an instant, at least—become one person.

And I had thought not a whit beyond that, it's true. I suspect that neither had she, and had I not created the opportunity for her to be alone in the bathroom, had we stayed together until we inevitably reached the bed, she would have been there with me still. I had, in my inimitable way, screwed everything up in the end. Probably, I thought, I could have convinced her to stay and sleep with me anyway—when I was younger I might have tried it—but in Nora's case I couldn't have lived with that. I would have felt like a murderer.

There was no use telling myself that her leaving was all for the best, that she'd go home and adjust to her life again and be kind to her (damn him!) husband, and that we would have made a sorry couple in the dreadful daylight of things, where our worlds would never have meshed, and where daily life could never have measured up to the pure exhilaration of our first meeting. I knew all that, and knew it to be all true, but it didn't help one bit.

Her last words echoed again and again in my head: "No right to become real for me," she'd said—or something like it. What in the bloody hell was real, though? Not much, in my experience; not even my first name was real. (For some idiotic reason I began to feel sadder than ever when I realized I'd not told Nora my real first name is James.)

And why had Nora accused me that way? She couldn't have meant it. Perhaps she did, but I didn't think so. And neither did I believe that I had really harmed her—no, even now I do not think I did. Neither of us was to blame. We were caught up in something, that's all, something private and shining gold and incredibly true. At one point in the afternoon, when I looked at Nora, I felt as though all my life I'd been standing in a darkened room, and my eyes had only just then become accustomed to the dimness, able to make out the shape of her, standing next to me all the time. If I would always miss her, I'd simply have to miss her—wasn't it better than never having known her at all? She'd given me back my youth and my interest in living; she'd given me mysteries to love and memories to dwell on, and one of the most tantalizing physical urges of my life—all the more precious for its unfulfillment. I was overwhelmed by my gratitude to her; I would use all this in my art. I wanted to give her something, something grand.

Which, I realized suddenly, was the impulse behind the object that had set this whole thing off: Nora's letter. I knew exactly where it was, and I thought, sentimentally (remember, I was quite drunk), of the words of a maudlin old song: "They can't take that away from me."And the drawing! I would always have the drawing Nora had made. I was luckier than she, poor duck, who'd gone away with nothing but a pair of enormous blue gloves. That thought made me laugh—how charmingly like her. Perhaps she would dust her books with them. Funny little witch.

My mind, too sick to walk a straight line, continued to wander.

I must have fallen asleep after a while, because the next thing I knew, Leon was hovering over me, holding his nose with one hand, slapping my cheek with the other, and saying, "Hugh, wake up, wake up," in a rasping, nasal voice.

I opened my eyes slightly. My head was immense. My tongue felt as if I had lowered it into a bowl of fiery salt.

"What do you want?" I growled.

Leon collapsed on the bed and sat there, breathing hard. "Good Lord, Hugh, I thought you were dead this time. I really couldn't wake you."

"Rubbish," I said. "As you can see, I'm quite awake."

"And naked, damp, and smelling like a barroom sink," he said, getting up and straightening the covers. "And smeared with cracker crumbs. . . and what on earth . . .?" he asked, just then spotting the flood on the floor.

"Nothing serious, Leon, an uncharted body of water, that's all," I said. "You can call for someone to mop it up someday." I turned over. "There's a good fellow." I realized the granite object I'd smacked my head upon was the pillow. I remembered Nora. I wanted to be unconscious again.

But Leon wouldn't let me. He drew back the drapes and I wailed at the brightness. It was morning. The sun, blast it, was burning away busily over Boston. I sat up. My back had a cutlass stuck in it, and it was slicing its way up from my waist toward my lungs and heart, making it painful to breathe. I imagined that soon it would lash into my old sutures and unleash a torrent of blood that would drown both Leon and me. I waited patiently for that to happen.

"And did you have a nice time with Miss Forrest?" Leon said, looking about the room for signs of her and barely masking his relief at not finding any.

"Oh, yes, I did indeed." I tried to smile at him brightly, but my face was paralyzed and far away. I could not seem to reach it, even with my hand. The voice I was using must have originated with some unseen ventriloquist in the room.

To my astonishment, Leon handed me a cup of coffee. "I don't approve," he said, "but in one hour we have a plane to catch. You know you have a performance tonight."

"Jesus, Mary, and Joseph," I moaned. The punishment simply did not fit the crime.

"You'll have to shave and shower," Leon told me, and pulled off all the covers.

I looked down at my body: a vast, lumpish fish, possibly a sturgeon. I prodded at my ribs with a finger, to see if they'd give, but they were still surprisingly solid. Leon pushed me into The Robe, put my slippers on my feet, handed me the coffee cup, and led me to the bathroom, where he arranged my shaving things and sat down to make sure I used them.

"Really, Hugh," he grumbled. "Really, I've never seen such a mess. You didn't even drain the tub." He did so then, and when I'd finished shaving, he put me into the shower, where I rubbed away more of my skin.

I felt a little better when I was dressed, and I asked Leon for more coffee, which he allowed me. He called for the car and went about gathering my things. I sat down carefully on the sofa, exactly where Nora had sat. I selected the spot for that reason. My heart was giving me a little trouble. It had a secret to protect.

"Leon, do you know about gillyflowers?" I knew he would. Leon loved gardens, knew things about buds and bugs and trees that often amazed me. He'd grown up under a wheelbarrow, I believed.

"What do you mean 'know about' them? Do you want a description?" Leon never seemed surprised by any inquiry of mine.

"I mean, I know what they are, but do you know anything strange about them, or. . . are there any legends surrounding them, or. . . ?" I depended on him to fill me in, though I didn't know what I was seeking.

"No particular legend that I know of. They're pretty little things, not all that common anymore. Part of the carnation family, I believe, although they grow quite wild. Some years ago I saw some when we were in Ireland. Lovely deep purply-pinkish color, like cows clover, you might say."

I looked at him. "They're yellow," I said. "A very pale shade."

"No, no," he countered, "for the most part they're pinkish-purple, or very rarely white, but come to think of it I believe I have heard of yellow gillyflowers, though I've never seen one. Expect they're rather rare."

"I've seen one, Leon. I saw one yesterday."

Leon was greatly pleased with me; he looked at me with a priceless affection in his baggy, doggy eyes. Not only was I offering no resistance to returning to New York, but I was engaging him in sensible, civilized conversation on one of his favorite topics.

"Really, Hugh, how nice! Did you find a botanical museum? You couldn't have seen it growing wild?"

"Quite wild, Leon. And quite lovely as well. My mother used to tell us we oughtn't pick them, so I didn't, but I wanted to tell you about it—I knew it would interest you."

"Yes, it is interesting. And you saw it growing wild. . . in Boston?"

I noted a touch of reluctant disbelief in his voice, like a child suspicious of Santa, but not willing to be disenchanted just yet. "There was a special place in the park." I checked his face for signs of guilt, but he gave no sign of being flustered. *Mere life experience*, I thought, *without a lick of deliberate study, has made of this Leon an actor greater than I.* Not only had he failed to betray his presence in the park the previous afternoon, he had not shown his disappointment at having missed what would have been to him a genuine treat of nature. Suddenly I felt sorry for tormenting him.

The call came that our car was waiting. We gathered our things and started out the door.I put my arm around Leon and kissed him on the cheek.

"You bloody fool," he said as we left the suite. "Don't start acting up now—we're in a hurry."

I turned for a moment and saw Nora curled up on the sofa. My heart stopped and started. She lifted a blue-gloved hand; it looked like a blessing. Leon gave me a little shove, and then he locked the door behind us.

Acknowledgments

My most affectionate thanks to Early James and my other first readers for their enthusiastic appraisal of and insightful comments on this manuscript.

And to Carey Reid, as always, for his love and unquestioning support in the face of my many mysteries.

About the Author

Diane Wald was born in Paterson, New Jersey, and has lived in Massachusetts since 1972. She holds a BA from Montclair State University and an MFA from the University of Massachusetts, Amherst. She has published more than 250 poems in literary magazines since 1966. She was the recipient of a two-year fellowship in poetry from the Fine Arts Work Center in Provincetown and has been awarded the Grolier Poetry Prize, The Denny Award, The Open Voice Award, and the Anne Halley Award. She also received a grant from the Artists Foundation (Massachusetts Council on the Arts). She has published four chapbooks (*Target of Roses* from Grande Ronde

Press, *My Hat That Was Dreaming* from White Fields Press, *Double Mirror* from Runaway Spoon Press, and *Faustinetta, Gegenschein, Trapunto* from Cervena Barva Press), and won the Green Lake Chapbook Award from Owl Creek Press. Her electronic chapbook (*Improvisations on Titles of Works by Jean Dubuffet*) appears on the *Mudlark* website. Her book *Lucid Suitcase* was published by Red Hen Press in 1999 and her second book, *The Yellow Hotel*, was published by Verse Press in the fall of 2002. *WONDERBENDER*, her third collection, was published by 1913 Press in 2011. She lives outside of Boston with her husband, Carey Reid, and their charismatic cats.

Selected Titles From She Writes Press

She Writes Press is an independent publishing company founded to serve women writers everywhere. Visit us at www.shewritespress.com.

Size Matters by Cathryn Novak. $16.95, 978-1-63152-103-4. If you take one very large, reclusive, and eccentric man who lives to eat, add one young woman fresh out of culinary school who lives to cook, and then stir in a love of musical comedy and fresh-brewed exotic tea, with just a hint of magic, will the result be a soufflé—or a charred, inedible mess?

The Geometry of Love by Jessica Levine. $16.95, 978-1-938314-62-9. Torn between her need for stability and her desire for independence, an aspiring poet grapples with questions of artistic inspiration, erotic love, and infidelity.

Conjuring Casanova by Melissa Rea. $16.95, 978-1-63152-056-3. Headstrong ER physician Elizabeth Hillman is a career woman who has sworn off men and believes the idea of love in the twenty-first century is a fairy-tale—but when Giacomo Casanova steps into her life on a rooftop in Italy, her reality and concept of love are forever changed.

The Rooms Are Filled by Jessica Null Vealitzek. $16.95, 978-1-938314-58-2. The coming-of-age story of two outcasts—a nine-year-old boy who just lost his father, and a closeted young woman—brought together by circumstance.

The End of Miracles by Monica Starkman. $16.95, 978-1-63152-054-9. When a pregnancy following years of infertility ends in late miscarriage, Margo Kerber sinks into a depression—one that leads her, when she encounters a briefly unattended baby, to commit an unthinkable crime.

Magic Flute by Patricia Minger. $16.95, 978-1-63152-093-8. When a car accident puts an end to ambitious flutist Liz Morgan's dreams, she returns to her childhood hometown in Wales in an effort to reinvent her path.